Sidekicks

THE BROTHERHOOD OF ROTTEN BABYSITTERS

Sidekicks
THE BROTHERHOOD OF ROTTEN BABYSITTERS

by Dan Danko and Tom Mason

Illustrated by Barry Gott

LITTLE, BROWN AND COMPANY

New York ✣ Boston

Little, Brown and Company

Time Warner Book Group

1271 Avenue of the Americas, New York, NY 10020

Visit our Web site at www.lb-kids.com

First Edition: June 2005

Library of Congress Cataloging-in-Publication Data

Danko, Dan.

The brotherhood of rotten babysitters / by Dan Danko and Tom Mason ;
illustrated by Barry Gott. — 1st ed.

p. cm. — (Sidekicks ; 5)

Summary: After Pumpkin Pete accidentally blows up the League of Big
Justice and the Sidekick Super Clubhouse, the superhero trouble begins.

ISBN 0-316-15895-X

[1. Heroes — Fiction. 2. Clubs — Fiction.] I. Title: Brotherhood of rotten
babysitters. II. Mason, Tom, 1958– III. Gott, Barry, ill. IV. Title.
V. Series: Danko, Dan. Sidekicks ; 5.

PZ7.D2285Br 2005

[Fic] — dc22   2004012220

10 9 8 7 6 5 4 3 2 1

RRC

Printed in the United States of America

The text for this book was set in Bookman Old Style,
and the display type is Bernhard Gothic Heavy Italic.
Series design by Billy Kelly.

To Amy Hsu —
thanks for laughing with us and not at us!

Chapter One
The Chapter That Begins This Book!

The explosion shook the walls and rattled the windows of the League of Big Justice. The vibration faded, and Pumpkin Pete scratched his large, orange chin.

"Hmmm. I guess it's not *that* button," he said, and hovered his finger over a different button.

"Uh, Pete," I said, "maybe we should wait until King Justice gets back before we push any more buttons?"

"Nonsense!" Pete blurted. "Buttons are made for pushing! If they weren't meant to be pushed, they'd be switches."

I know that made perfect sense to Pete. But then, filling his head with whipped cream and running around yelling "I'm pumpkin pie! I'm pumpkin pie!" also makes sense to Pete. He claims it's a trap to see who really wants to eat him.

"I know one of these days, one of those creepy kids in Spandex is going to come after me with a fork and a tub of Cool Whip," Pete once said to me as he squirted the whipped cream up his hollow nose.

"'Creepy kids in Spandex?'" I asked. "You mean the *Sidekicks*?"

"Is *that* what they are? Well, when Stabby the Fork Boy comes after me with his Super Fork, I'll be ready for his forky ways!" Pete shook his fist in defiance, then mumbled, "Curse you, Stabby . . ."

"Who's Stabby the Fork Boy?" I asked, realizing that the answer would probably leave me even more confused.

"He's the kid in purple Spandex that runs around with that fork yelling 'It's stabbin' time!'" Pete replied as whipped cream started to ooze out his ears.

See, I'm a superhero sidekick. My code name is Speedy (real name: Guy Martin). I can run over 100 miles per hour. Pumpkin Pete is my superhero sponsor, and I'm at the Sidekick Super Clubhouse every day. I've never seen any kid in purple

Spandex running around with a fork, yelling "It's stabbin' time!" Although, there was that *one* time Boom Boy ran around the Clubhouse with a cardboard box over his head and a trombone in his hand, shouting, "Everybody make way for Boxy the Trombone Boy! Toot! Toot!"

I'm still trying to figure out what *that* was all about.

But right now, I had to figure out who had sent the large, crazy-looking machine to the League of Big Justice, and how I could stop Pete from pushing more of its buttons.

"You *do* realize that these buttons are blowing things up every time you push one?" I pointed out.

"And don't you think switches blow things up? You've got a lot to learn if you don't think switches are every bit as evil as buttons!" Pete's long, viney finger poked another button. An explosion echoed in the distance. "And now my keen pumpkin senses have detected a second button not to push!"

"I really, really, really think it's a very, very, very bad idea to keep pushing buttons."

Pete spun away from the machine and glared at me. "Let me tell you something about superheroes, Spuddy . . ."

"Speedy," I corrected.

"Whatever. Now the thing about superheroes is, we're super! And because we are super, we do super things. And super things are . . . uh . . . they're . . . uh . . ."

"Super?" I offered.

"You bet your pumpkin pie they're super! That's why we're *super*heroes! And I assure you, as a superhero, all the things I do are *super*!" Pete snarled. "Super! Super! SUPER!"

"Uh . . . what's your point?" I asked.

"I have no idea!" Pete shouted back. "Now get out of my way so I can push more buttons!"

Pete slapped his palm on a large button near the top of the machine. There was a moment of silence, and then the Sidekick Super Clubhouse exploded.

"Pete! You blew up our clubhouse!" I said accusingly.

"Eh, that thing was blocking my view of Crosscreek Park anyway," Pete defended as Sidekick Super Clubhouse debris rained down on the League of Big Justice Parking Lot of Big Justice.

"Super," I said, and dropped my head into my hands.

Chapter Two
The Chapter That Continues the Story!

Pete nudged a glazed doughnut that lay next to his foot. He looked at the smoldering ruins where the Sidekick Super Clubhouse once stood and sighed. He tilted his head slightly so he could better see the smoldering ruins of Crosscreek Park. The twelfth button Pete pushed blew up the park, to which Pete had responded, "Eh, that park was blocking my view of Donutz Village."

The thirteenth button Pete pushed had blown up Donutz Village and sent a rain of Cinnabuns and jelly-filled, powdered, and sprinkle-covered doughnuts across the League of Big Justice Parking Lot of Big Justice.

Pete picked up a burnt sugar doughnut.

"Hungry?" he said, and offered me the blackened breakfast treat. I shook my head no.

"What're we going to do, Pete?" I asked. We were lucky no one got hurt from all the button pushing and explosions.

Pete took a bite of the charred doughnut. "Well . . . did I mention I was super?"

"Yes." I sighed.

Pete's face contorted and his nose wrinkled. He spit out a black wad of sugar doughnut. "And that doughnut is anything *but* super!" He held the doughnut out to me again. "Are you sure you don't want it?"

"*Yes,*" I repeated.

Pete shrugged and stuffed the rest of the doughnut into his mouth and chewed with a painful expression of displeasure.

"If it's so bad, why are you eating it?" I asked.

Pete pulled another scorched doughnut from under some burnt leaves. "Free food," he mumbled, and stuffed the second doughnut into his mouth.

"Ahoy, fearsome fighters of the good fight!" It was King Justice, the coolest superhero ever to squeeze into Spandex and the leader of the League of Big Justice. He drove his Super Minivan of Kid Transport and Soccer Equipment around a large piece of burning rubble and pulled up next to Pete and me. On the bumper of his car was a sticker that read #1 SOCCER DAD. King Justice climbed from the car and surveyed the destruction.

"I didn't do it!" Pete immediately said.

"You're probably wondering what happened," I stated.

"Wondering what happened," King Justice began, "or wondering what evil forces could be responsible for the destruction of so many yummy doughnuts?!"

Pete stuffed two more burnt doughnuts into his mouth. "Miff ma fwa bwaah hwo ga maff," he explained, doughnuts packed into his cheeks.

King Justice looked at me, as if I'd know what the heck Pete was saying. I shrugged. "I guess it all began when this machine showed up at the League of Big Justice Hall of Big Justice."

King Justice scanned the area. "And speaking of the League of Big Justice Hall of Big Justice . . . where is it exactly?"

I looked to the place where the Hall of Big Justice used to be. There was a high pile of rubble and several small fires.

"Let me tell you about the fourteenth button Pete pushed . . ."

"Buttons?" King Justice gasped. "Does evil have no shame?! Does it know our *every* weakness?! Buttons are made! To! Be! Pushed! Who can resist the call of a BIG! RED! JUICY! BUTTON?!" King Justice grabbed his head as if the very thought of a big red button was driving him insane. "The very thought of a big red button is driving! Me! Insane!"

Pumpkin Pete leaned over to me. "I told you," he said.

"The only thing that could have made this plan more evil is a plan with switches! You should see the things switches blow up!" King Justice gasped.

"Told you again," Pete said to me. He jumped up from the curb and ran over to a cream puff that had a little flame still flickering on top. "Look! It's like a little birthday cake! A little birthday cake that blew up and landed in my parking lot!"

King Justice moved a chunk of burning leather that used to be his La-Z-Boy chair and sat on the curb next to me. "Well, on the bright side, we don't have to give any more tours. Oh! The questions I had to answer! My head! Pounding!"

Unless he was strapped to a rocket and being blasted into the heart of the sun or something,

King Justice always took a few hours every weekend to give tours of the League of Big Justice Hall of Big Justice. After the tour, he always had a question-and-answer session. You'd think that if people had the chance to ask a question, any question, to the superhero responsible for saving the Earth about a hundred times, they'd ask better questions than "Can you create a rock that you can't crush?"

After the guy had asked that question, King Justice considered his answer carefully. "I . . . I can't create rocks," he finally replied.

"You can't? Oh." The man also took a moment to think. "But I'm just saying, like, if you *could* create a rock, could you create one that you can't crush?"

Another boy raised his hand. "King Justice! King Justice! In episode 42 of *Alias*, why did Sydney allow Sark to escape when she knew he was working with the Covenant?"

King Justice shuffled a foot and turned an embarrassed shade of red.

"Uh . . . I don't know. I don't watch that TV show," he confessed.

"It's not a TV show!" the kid yelled back. "It's *Alias*!"

"If you were on an deserted island, which

superhero would you vote off first?" a girl called out.

King Justice puffed out his chest. This was an *easy* question. "I wouldn't vote anyone off. I'd build a large platform for everyone to stand on, then help The Librarian to fly us off the island."

"You can't fly off the island . . . unless it's an Immunity Challenge," the girl corrected him.

Small beads of sweat formed on King Justice's brow. "An . . . Immunity Challenge?" he wondered aloud. King Justice looked to the door, probably hoping it would blast off its hinges and a supervillain would come and strap him to a rocket and blast him into the heart of the sun.

Or something.

Chapter Three
The Chapter in Which Even More Stuff Happens!

"Hey! Hey! Who ordered doughnuts?" Boom Boy asked as he strolled up to the curb. King Justice was gone, picking through the rubble of the League of Big Justice Headquarters of Big Justice while Pumpkin Pete wandered about the parking lot collecting doughnuts and any loose change he could find.

"No one ordered doughnuts," I explained.

"What? What? They just fell from the sky?" Boom Boy replied.

"Yeah. Kind of. After Pete blew up Donutz Village, it just kind of started raining doughnuts."

Pete looked up. He was on the other side of the League of Big Justice Parking Lot of Big

Parking with an armful of chocolate-frosted doughnuts and a fistful of change. "I didn't do it!" he shouted.

"Wait a second! You're saying that you blew up Donutz Village without me?" Boom Boy blurted out.

"What do you mean, without you? It's not like Pete and I got together and said 'Hey! Let's blow up Donutz Village, but not invite Boom Boy.' Pete blew it up by accident. I think."

"So that's how it's going to be, huh? You think you can just go and blow up Donutz Village without Boom Boy?" Boom Boy snarled and balled his fists. "All those months of planning! Ruined! Those doughnuts should be mine, I tell you! Mine! I'll show you what happens when you blow up Donutz Village without Boom Boy!"

With that, he stepped back from the curb and balled his fists. His face grew redder and redder as he prepared to blow himself up.

"Why's Boom Boy trying to blow himself up?" Exact Change Kid asked. It was time for the daily sidekicks meeting and soon all of them would be here.

"Because we blew up Donutz Village without him," I explained.

Boom Boy doubled over and grunted loudly. His face grew more and more red.

"What?! You blew up Donutz Village?" Exact Change Kid cried out. He pulled out his notebook from his utility belt and flipped to the middle. He tore out several pages and threw them at my feet. "All those months of planning! Ruined! Those doughnuts should be mine!"

I picked up one crumpled piece of paper. Across the top it read in large block letters: OPERATION DONUTZ VILLAGE. Below that it read in smaller letters: OBJECTIVE: TOTAL DONUT SUPREMACY. The other pages were filled with schematics, arrows, formulas, and a two-hundred-step plan to get all the doughnuts from Donutz Village.

The last page was a poorly drawn picture of Exact Change Kid sitting atop a mountain of doughnuts. Above his head was a banner that read KING DONUT.

Exact Change Kid doubled over and grunted loudly. His face grew more and more red as he and Boom Boy both clenched their fists tighter and gritted their teeth.

"What are you doing?" I said to Exact Change Kid. "You can't blow yourself up!"

"I . . . know," grunted Exact Change Kid

between clenched teeth. "But right . . . now I'm . . . so . . . mad . . . I wish . . . I could!"

"If you guys want free doughnuts so badly, just go get some! They're all over the place!" I pointed out. Suddenly Pete increased his pace of doughnut collecting, as if he knew competition was on its way.

"Wait!" Boom Boy said, and opened his eyes. "I get it now. I get it. You *want* me to blow up don't you? Yeah. 'Cause once I do, I'll be gone and then there'll be more free doughnuts for you."

"But I don't want any of the doughnuts," I informed him.

"And that's how it better stay, because if you do, I swear, I swear I'll blow myself up!"

"Yeah! I swear I'll blow myself up, too!" Exact Change Kid threatened.

I dropped my head into my hands. Right about now I really wish one of those big buttons had blown *me* up.

"Maaa pam mam maa pah ma mam pamh mam?" Boy-in-the-Plastic-Bubble Boy asked as he rolled up in his Giant Hamster Ball of Justice. Large doughnuts were flattened all around the outside. The clear shell of his hamster ball looked as if it had acne.

Chocolate acne with pink and yellow sprinkles.

"You'll never guess," Exact Change Kid said. "Speedy blew up Donutz Village."

"MAAA PAM MA MA PAAA!? MA!? MA-HA-HA-HAAAAAH!" Boy-in-the-Plastic-Bubble Boy yelled, and ran forward so fast he hit his forehead against the inside of his Giant Hamster Ball of Justice and slid down the inside like a big, pink hairless hamster who had just found out his favorite doughnut shop had been blown up by a guy with a pumpkin for a head.

"Technically, *I* didn't blow it up," I corrected.

"It's a little too late for apologies now," Boom Boy grumbled. He peeled a squished doughnut from the side of Boy-in-the-Plastic-Bubble Boy's Giant Hamster Ball of Justice, sniffed it once, shrugged his shoulders, and took a bite.

Boy-in-the-Plastic-Bubble Boy sat at the bottom of his giant ball and let out a sad whimper. He pulled a small, crumbled piece of paper from his utility belt and stared at it as if it were an old photograph. I could see only the top of the worn piece of paper.

PROJECT DONUTZ VILLAGE, it said.

"Did you guys hear?!" Spelling Beatrice yelled as she and Spice Girl raced up. "Someone blew up Donutz Village!!"

"Someone . . . ?" Boom Boy asked in a sarcastic tone, and kicked me with his toe.

"Do you know how much more sad I could be right now?" Spice Girl asked. "None more. That's how much more."

I sat on the curb and watched Boom Boy and Exact Change Kid join Pumpkin Pete in his doughnut collecting. Boy-in-the-Plastic-Bubble Boy sat in the bottom of his Giant Hamster Ball of Justice and stared blankly at the failed ambitions of "Project Donutz Village." King Justice returned with the broken left arm of his statue from the destroyed Hall of Heroes of Big Justice, and Spelling Beatrice quietly looked around the area.

"Where's the Sidekick Super Clubhouse?" she finally asked.

All the other sidekicks froze. They joined Spelling Beatrice in her search and then, one by one, they turned and glared at me. I dropped my head into my hands, wishing that a supervillain would come and strap me to a rocket and blast me into the heart of the sun.

Or something.

Chapter Four
The Chapter That Is Not About Doughnuts

"I really, really, really, really think this is a terrible idea!" I said to my mom again, but this time I added a fourth "really" because three "reallys" just didn't seem to faze her.

And don't think I'm not desperate enough to use five "reallys." Someone much smarter than me and much more dead once said, "Desperate times call for more reallys." Or something like that. I wasn't paying very much attention in class that day.

"It's the least I could do," my mom explained. "After all, you *did* blow up their secret fort."

"It wasn't a secret fort, and I didn't blow it up!" I defended.

"Don't talk back to your mother," Pumpkin Pete said, and closed the refrigerator door. He had a POW! soda in one hand and last night's leftover meatloaf in the other. He tossed the meatloaf into the microwave, popped open the top on the POW! soda, leaned against the kitchen counter, and asked, "So, this dump get cable TV, or what?"

I grabbed my mom by the arm and led her from the kitchen. I moved her through the living room and past King Justice, who was eagerly pushing a vacuum across the carpet.

"Flee before my sucking might, villainous dust bunnies!" King Justice yelled, and jabbed the vacuum hose under the couch. The long vacuum extension looked like a slender toothpick in his massive, heroic hands. "Your grime! Spree! Is! Over!"

"Mom? Why is King Justice wearing an apron?"

"He didn't want to get his Spandex dirty," she said in a matter-of-fact tone, as if there was nothing more natural than Earth's greatest superhero draped in an apron that had KISS THE COOK emblazoned across the front in letters shaped like carrots and broccoli.

I led my mom to the bathroom and closed the

door. "I know the League of Big Justice Hall of Justice was blown up, but do you really think it's a good idea to let them use our house as a temporary headquarters?" I asked.

My mom thought for a moment. "Well . . . it *is* just temporary. And I told them they weren't allowed in your room. I know how embarrassing you think that is."

Embarrassing? I'll tell you what embarrassing is. Embarrassing is wearing brightly colored Spandex. Embarrassing is when that brightly colored Spandex creeps up your butt and you're dying to pick it out, but you're in the middle of a grand opening ceremony for a new supermarket and are surrounded by ten thousand people with cameras. Embarrassing is when you're surfing the Web a few days later and find out that one of those ten thousand people with a camera followed you around the corner and took a photo while you "secretly" did a little Spandex-picking. Embarrassing is when the other sidekicks start calling you "Picky" for a week. *That's* embarrassing.

Having your mom drive up in the car while you sit on the curb in front of a mountain of rubble that *used* to be the League of Big Justice Hall of Justice and then offer to let the League of

Big Justice use your home as their headquarters until the rubble is cleared out is *not* embarrassing.

It's the most humiliating day in your life is what it is.

At first King Justice had turned down my mom's "generous offer to use her humble and common two-story domicile to house the greatest good the world has ever known." But then Pete pulled out the League of Big Justice Super Emergency Manual for Really Bad Emergencies and read aloud, "In the event of a really bad emergency" — here he looked at the smoking ruins of Donutz Village — "in the event of a really bad emergency, protocol calls for the League of Big Justice . . ." he lowered the book again and stated, "That would be us," then returned to reading, ". . . the League of Big Justice to convene at the most immediately available location, especially if said location is supplied by the Sidekick responsible for blowing up Donutz Village in the first place." He slammed the book shut with a triumphant nod. "So it's settled!"

"WHAT?!" I exploded. "It doesn't say that!"

"Well, maybe not *that* exactly, but it's the basic gist. More or less." Pete shrugged.

And so there we were, the League of Big

Justice doing yard work, the Sidekicks laughing at me, and Pumpkin Pete eating everything that wasn't nailed down.

"But what if evil attacks? Did you ever think about that?" I asked my mom as we stood in the bathroom.

"Honey, the best place to hide an egg is in the chicken coop," she replied.

"What? I don't even know what that means!"

My mom opened the bathroom door and headed out. "You can use that super speed of yours to run around evil invasions and death rays, but you can't use it to run around life."

"Couldn't you at least wear the Identity Containment Apparatus like you did at the League of Big Justice Family Picnic of Egg Salad or whatever that thing was called?" I thrust the ICA unit into my mom's hands.

"You want me to wear a paper bag over my head in my *own house*?" my mom huffed.

"It's not just a paper bag," I quickly pointed out, hoping to convince her it wasn't just a paper bag, which would be rather difficult because it *was* just a paper bag. "It's an Identity Containment Apparatus designed specifically to protect your identity and make sure that no supervillain knows you're related to —"

"Yes, yes. I remember that bearded, kilt-wearing man's speech at the picnic that day when he made your father and me put bags on our heads. Although I couldn't really understand much of what he was saying . . . especially all that nonsense about 'tree rats.'"

"His name is Captain Haggis," I reminded her. At least stop making them do all these chores!" I called after her. "I mean . . . they're *superheroes.*"

She stopped in the hallway and turned. "Just because they've fought aliens and saved the planet from destruction doesn't mean they don't have to earn their keep in *my* house. I don't care if they have the power of mimedom or can throw all the pennies in the world. As long as they're under my roof, they live by my rules."

"Hear! Hear!" Pumpkin Pete called out. He fell back onto the couch, plopped his long, slender legs onto our coffee table, and shoveled a large forkful of blueberry pie into his fat orange mouth.

Chapter Five
This Chapter Is Not About Doughnuts, Either.
Although Someone May THINK About Doughnuts!

"And this one was taken when Guy was nine. He just tripped and dumped that whole bowl of Jell-O right on his head!"

"Hoooph! Hoooph! Hoooph!" The muffled sound came from Boy-in-the-Plastic-Bubble Boy. I *think* he was laughing. Either that, or he was really a robot and his head had just fallen off and tumbled down a deep hole. With Boy-in-the-Plastic-Bubble Boy, you could never be too sure. "Hoooph! Hoooph! Hoooph!"

The rest of the Sidekicks laughed as well. They were huddled around my mom like cold pioneers gathered around a warm fire, except the only warm glow the Sidekicks were basking in was the burning heat of my deep humiliation — humiliation that was so bad, it was like embarrassment wrapped in shame wrapped in mortification wrapped in disgrace wrapped in a corn dog and dipped in ketchup while being eaten by some chubby kid with dirt on his face and a bad hair cut.

"Oh! And here's one of my favorites! One day Guy just decided to dress up in my favorite —"

"Okay, mom! I think they've seen enough!" I said and tried to turn the page. I've fought madmen and crazy scientists, but I could tell this was going to be my greatest battle ever. Those other villains paled in comparison to the threat of a proud mother with baby photos.

My life was over.

"Oh, Guy! Don't be such a party pooper!" my mom interjected and gently tugged the photo album back.

"We fought him once. He was stinky," Spice Girl volunteered.

"That was Le Poop," Spelling Beatrice corrected.

"The Party Pooper changed his name to Le Poop?" Spice Girl asked.

"The Party Pooper was named Le Poop."

"His real name was Le Poop? Who would name their child Le Poop? I'll bet the kids picked on him all the time. 'Look! Look! It's Le Poop-a-Doop!'" Spice Girl sadly shook her head. "Poor Le Poop."

Spelling Beatrice rolled her eyes. "The guy we fought had the supervillain name of Le Poop. I don't know his real name."

"Then who's the Party Pooper?" Spice Girl questioned.

"Speedy is!" Boom Boy laughed.

Spice Girl scratched her head. "If Speedy's the Party Pooper, then who was the guy who farted a lot?"

"That was Commander Farto: The Human Stink Bomb," Exact Change Kid reminded her.

"You kids fight a lot of smelly people," my mom commented.

"That's because evil *is* smelly," Exact Change Kid replied. "And evil."

"And rude," Spice Girl added. "But if you ask me, evil just didn't get enough hugs as a child. I think the next time we fight someone who's trying to blow up the world, instead of punching them in the face, we should probably just give them a biiiig hug and listen to what they have to say. Unless they're stinky."

"You're a very wise sidekick," my mom said. "Are you the leader?"

"Only during cheers," Spice Girl giggled, then added a loud "Goooo team!"

"You're nuts!" I said, glad that the Sidekicks' attention was diverted from my baby photos. "You can't solve the world's problems by giving evil a hug!"

"Mostly because it's so farty," Spice Girl explained to my mom.

"No! You can't hug evil, because it's evil!" I began.

"*And* farty," Spice Girl stressed.

"Evil doesn't like hugs. Evil's got killer robots and master plans! Evil wants to invade and rule the world! It wants to crush us under its evil heel or make us work in its evil salt mines!" I was on a roll. I stood up from the couch and bumped the plate of Ritz Crackers and Hi-C juice packs my mom had put out for snacks. "Evil doesn't like to fly kites! It doesn't like birthdays or puppies —"

"Except for *evil* puppies," Boom Boy cut in. "And I think they'd like flying kites if a death ray was attached to them."

"No! No it would not! And do you know why?!" I asked.

"Because it never got hugs when it was a child?" Spice Girl offered.

"No. Because it's EVIL! And it won't stop until it's destroyed everything good in this world! It won't stop until everything that makes this life worth living is ruined and in flames! *That's* why it's evil!"

The Sidekicks all looked at each other in silence.

"You sure are a downer sometimes, Speedy," Boom Boy said, and sucked on his grape Hi-C pack. He leaned over to my mom and added, "He's kind of like this all the time, you know."

"That's why we call him 'Party Pooper,'" Spice Girl added.

My mom considered Boom Boy's words. "Maybe . . . maybe I should hug him more?"

"Yes, you should!" Spice Girl agreed. "And the world would be a much better place!"

Pumpkin Pete walked up. "Hey, who's the dorky kid wearing the woman's dress?" he asked, looking over my mom's shoulder at the photo album that rested in her lap.

"Oh, that's Guy!" My mom laughed.

"Guy? Who's Guy?" Pumpkin Pete asked.

"Speedy. It's Speedy," Boom Boy explained.

Pete reached a long, vincy arm over the couch

and grabbed a Hi-C juice pack. He stabbed the little straw into the top and sipped. "Who's Speedy?"

"Me," I said. I couldn't believe my deep sense of humiliation could get any worse, but I had a rotten suspicion it was about to.

"You? I thought your name was Picky," Pete replied.

"No. My name is Speedy."

Pete slightly closed one large eye, as if he was summing up the situation. He took a hard suck on his juice pack. "If your name is Speedy, then why do you always answer when I call you Picky?"

"I'll bet his real name is Le Poop," Spice Girl whispered to Spelling Beatrice.

"I answer when you call me 'Picky' for the same reason I answer you when you call me 'Spuddy' and 'Spotty' and 'Spammy' and 'My Human Bulletproof Shield' and 'Potato.'"

"Hey, Le Poop!" Spice Girl waited a moment, but I didn't respond. "Just checking," she said.

"The reason I answer you when you call me 'Picky,'" I began again, "is because no matter how many times I tell you my real sidekick name is *Speedy,* you either don't know it or don't care, so I might as well answer you no matter what you call me."

Pete looked at me and shoved a handful of Ritz Crackers in his mouth. "Wow. Looks like someone didn't get enough hugs as a kid."

Chapter Six
We've Run Out of Chapter Titles, So We'll Just Call This One "Mikey"!

I headed out to the backyard. Just when I thought things couldn't get any worse, my mom had gathered the Sidekicks in the kitchen for "training."

"When making a salad, always remember to peel the carrot *away* from you," my mom had said, and slid the peeler along the carrot's orange skin. "And never run with scissors."

That was all I needed to hear. I took the photo album, and anything else my mother might use to torture me, hid them under my bed, and then headed outside.

It was a beautiful day; the kind of day you would never think began with Pumpkin Pete pushing buttons on a mysterious machine sent to the League of Big Justice until he pretty much blew up everything around us. No, usually the days when Pete blows things up or accidentally disintegrates something are cloudy. I don't know why. It just seems to work out that way.

The Good Egg was in the front yard mowing the lawn and Ms. Mime was using imaginary hedge clippers to trim an imaginary hedge. Or maybe it was a bush. I don't know. It was imaginary.

I guess on the bright side, all my chores were being done for me — and by the world's greatest superheroes, no less.

I strolled to the backyard. Mr. Ironic was watering the container plants with a hose. "I've got a real green thumb!" he boasted, not realizing the plants he was watering were fake.

Or did he?

Then I heard a noise in the bushes. Something was in there. Something big. I moved closer. The tall, thick row of undergrowth lined the back wall like a small, wild jungle. It would be the perfect hiding place for evil as it plotted and planned to invade my house and fight the League of Big Justice . . . and my mother. I slowly crept up to the thicket and heard the cracking of dead leaves and branches. "Aaack!" a voice cried out from inside.

"Come out!" I called back. "I know you're in there!" I dropped back a few feet and stood in my battle stance, ready for whatever was about to leap out at me.

"Aye! Boyo!" Captain Haggis shouted as he stumbled from the thicket. His kilt was torn. Broken twigs and leaves were stuck to his beard. His chest heaved with each deep breath. His eyes were wild, as if panic clenched his half-crazed mind. "Yew've got ta 'elp me, laddie!"

"What is it?! Are we under attack?!" I gasped.

"Aye! By the nastiest tree rat yew ever did see!" Captain Haggis panted. "Yer ma sent me oot 'ere t'me doom! She tricked me, she did! Tol' me theh be weeds that need pullin'! An' look what ah've got ta deal with!" Captain Haggis stabbed a finger at the impenetrable undergrowth. "Me Bagpipes a' MacMcTarrganonnin e' still be in theh somewheh! What good be a Scotsman withoot his bag, laddie?" Captain Haggis turned to face the dense bushes. He pulled back two thick, leafy branches and stuck his head inside.

"Uh . . . Captain Haggis? What's a tree rat?"

He spun from the undergrowth. "Whar be th' foul li'l critter? Do ya see 'im, laddie?" He spun in various directions, poised and ready for any possible attack. "Whar is he?! WHAR?!"

"I haven't seen him. In fact, I don't even know what a tree rat is."

"Don't knew what a tree rat is?! Och! I'll tell yeh this, laddie — they be th' foulest vermin knewn, with them li'l beedy eyes an' them teeth jus' gnawin' at yer very suul! They be not a' this earth, I'll tell yew that!" He bent two of his fingers and raked them at me to show me how the tree rat gnawed his very suul — I mean soul.

Just then, Captain Haggis froze. His eyes grew wide, like the wide eyes of a bearded Scotsman without his bagpipes who felt the tree rat gnawing at his very soul. His muscles tensed and his eyes slowly moved down toward his beard.

"Whatever yew dew, don't move, laddie . . ."

Just then, something burst from Captain Haggis's thick, bushy beard. It was brown and furry with a bushy tail. It hit the ground and bolted toward the nearest tree.

"Thar she be!" Captain Haggis shouted, and dove toward the small animal. "Yew'll not get away fr'm Cap'n 'aggis this time, yew foul tree rat!"

The little animal let out a panicked squeal and raced up the tree. Captain Haggis balled his massive fists and punched the mighty oak. "Yew'll not get away fr'm me so easily, furry l'il bandit!"

"Uh . . . Captain Haggis . . ."

"Not now, laddie! I'm punchin' th' tree!"

"But . . . uh . . . the . . ." Bark flew off in shattered chunks.

He stopped punching and gritted his teeth. Captain Haggis took a step back and shook an angry fist at the small squirrel, which had long since hidden himself deep within the oak's branches. "This batt'l goes to yew, tree rat! But Cap'n 'aggis 'as yet ta give up th' war!" He turned from the tree and stomped back toward the thick undergrowth. His cheeks flushed red. "I'll say this much: Them foul critters dew make fine eatin' tho!" he said as he disappeared into the undergrowth, in search of his lost Bagpipes a' MacMcTarrganonnin.

I headed back to the house. Sure, a nightmare combination of my mom with baby photos and the best way to dice celery awaited me, but it was either that or help Depression Dave rake leaves. And trust me when I say, you do not want to help Depression Dave do *anything.*

"Why bother raking them?" Depression Dave had said the moment I walked up with a garbage bag. "I mean, the trees'll just make more and we'll have to do the whole thing over again. I mean, if we really wanted to end the leaf problem, we should probably just cut the trees down."

"Och! When yew dew, the tree rat is mine!" Captain Haggis shouted from somewhere deep in the undergrowth.

"Cutting trees down depresses me." Depression Dave sighed. His shoulders slumped slightly and he halfheartedly dragged the rake across the leaves. He stopped for a moment and looked up at the tree. A lone leaf broke from a high branch. It fell for a few moments, then a gust of wind caught it and swept it into the sky. Depression Dave watched the leaf grow smaller and smaller as it blew farther away and disappeared into the great blue sky.

"*Pfff.* Welcome to my life," Depression Dave groaned.

"What . . . uh . . . what powers do you *have,* exactly?" I asked. I had always wondered, but somehow never knew exactly the right way to ask . . . or if I should even ask. Ever.

"Powers? What powers do any of us have? What powers did these leaves have when they fell from the tree and waited to be raked up and thrown away?" He dropped the rake in the middle of the leaf pile and stared blankly at it. "Ask the rake. That's who you should be asking, 'What powers do you have?'"

I took a few slow steps toward the house.

"Uh, yeah. I'm going back to planet Earth for a little while. I'll see you when you land."

Back in the house, the Sidekicks were helping my mom make chocolate chip cookies. Spice Girl had arranged all her chocolate chips to make a happy face on a cookie, but when the cookie came out of the oven, she wouldn't let anyone eat it.

"How can you eat something that's smiling at you?" she asked, grabbing the cookie away from Spelling Beatrice.

Exact Change Kid finished stirring the final bowl of batter. He pulled out the large wooden spoon, and just as he was about to lick the cookie dough globbed to the top, Boom Boy grabbed it from his hand.

"We all get a lick!" Boom Boy declared.

"But I was the one who did all the stirring!" Exact Change Kid protested. "Everyone knows the person who does the stirring gets to lick the spoon. It's the reward for all the hard work."

"Hard work?! It's cookie batter!" Boom Boy snorted.

Exact Change Kid snagged the spoon from Boom Boy. "I stirred! I get to lick!"

Boom Boy curled his lip. "If you take one lick, I swear I'll . . . I'll . . ."

"You'll do what?" Exact Change Kid asked. He narrowed his eyes and glared at Boom Boy.

"I'll blow myself up!" Boom Boy yelled.

"I think he's serious. You better give him the spoon," Spice Girl warned.

Exact Change Kid gritted his teeth. He slowly extended the cookie dough spoon to Boom Boy, then quickly pulled it back and took a big lick of the cookie dough clumped on top.

"That does it!" Boom Boy shouted. "I'm blowing up!"

Boom Boy balled his fists and doubled over as Exact Change Kid licked the spoon with even more zeal.

"What's going on here?" my mom asked, entering the kitchen.

"Boom Boy's going to blow himself up because Exact Change Kid won't share the cookie dough stuck on the spoon," I explained.

"I stirred! I should get to lick!" Exact Change Kid whined. He clutched the spoon tightly against his chest, the gooey cookie dough sticking to the Spandex.

"As long as you're under my roof, you'll live by my rules," my mom declared. "And I say there's no blowing up in *my* house!"

Boom Boy looked up, shocked he wasn't

being allowed to blow up. "But . . . but . . . ," he stammered.

"Butts are on horses and cigarettes," my mom interrupted. "Now maybe some supervillain stitching together an army of the undead from dug-up body parts may not care if you go around blowing up their kitchens, but *I* do! I just mopped this floor and I'll be as angry as a honey bee in a bear's mouth if I have to spend the rest of my weekend scrubbing *you* off the ceiling!"

"Honey bee in a bear's mouth?" Spelling Beatrice whispered to me.

"Don't ask," I said.

"Now you stop trying to blow up this instant!" my mom demanded, and twisted Boom Boy's ear. "Or there'll be no cookies for you!"

"Even the ones that aren't smiling!" Spice Girl added. She crossed her arms.

Boom Boy stopped trying to blow up. He pursed his lips and stared at the ground. "I'm sorry, Speedy's mom."

"And you," my mom continued, turning on Exact Change Kid. "Don't you think Abe Lincoln shared his logs? Or that George Washington shared the bananas from that tree he chopped down? Why, FDR created the Lend-Lease program just to help England bomb people. The next time you throw your little coins at evil's face, maybe you better stop for a moment and ask yourself, 'What would those presidential heads have done with their cookie dough spoon?'"

"I know! I know!" Spice Girl thrust her hand in the air and jumped up and down. "They wouldn't have done anything because they have no arms and are made of metal!"

"Maybe baking cookies is a challenge you sidekicks aren't ready for," my mom continued.

"Mom! We fight supervillains!" I laughed.

"Well, lucky for me it wasn't a cookie supervillain." She took the cookie dough spoon from Exact Change Kid and laid it on the counter. "Otherwise I'd be in peanut butter shackles and snickerdoodle chains."

All the Sidekicks hung their heads in shame; the kind of shame that went hand in hand with a planet enslaved by cookie overlords and forced to wear peanut butter shackles and snickerdoodle chains.

"Did someone say snickerdoodles?!" Pumpkin Pete cried out as he skidded into the kitchen. He looked at the somber sidekicks, then spotted the doughy spoon. In one quick motion, he snatched it from the countertop and shoved the entire thing into his fat, pumpkin mouth. "Got any milk in this dump?" he asked, completely oblivious to the sad whimper of defeat that leaked from Exact Change Kid's mouth.

A sad whimper of defeat that meant, "Hey, *you* didn't stir."

"First Donutz Village and now this," Boom Boy groaned.

That's when my house started to shake.

Chapter Eight
He Likes It! Mikey Likes It!

"I hope it's not a cookie invasion!" Spice Girl cried, "or we're all doomed!"

I rushed to my mom's side and protected her from pans that fell from a nearby cupboard. "It's an earthquake!" she shouted.

"Everyone drop and roll!" Spice Girl added.

"That's for fires!" I yelled out over the loud rumbling.

"There's a fire?!" Exact Change Kid yelped.

"Quick! Get the hose!" Boom Boy called out, and raced for the front door.

Suddenly, as quickly as it started, the violent shaking stopped. I had never experienced an earthquake before, at least not one that wasn't caused by some giant earthquake ray or the King of the Tunnel People using the earth's molten core to cause havoc for the "surface dwellers."

That's one thing I've noticed about kings from under the earth or sea. They always call us "surface dwellers" and are always causing havoc. They always want to invade and crush the "surface dwellers." I mean, you'll never catch me leading an army underground shouting "crush the tunnel dwellers." Who wants to live underground, anyway? But then, I guess that's just why they're always trying to crush us.

What is it with races that live *under* things; like under the sea or the earth? And why do they like havoc so much? Sure, *sometimes* they'll cause chaos, but nine times out of ten, it's havoc. You may *think* that "chaos" and "havoc" are the same thing, but trust me when I say there are subtle differences that set the villain apart from the *super*villain.

"Uh, Speedy? Maybe you should come take a look at this," Boom Boy said, returning to the kitchen.

"If it's Captain Haggis fighting a 'tree rat,' I know all about it," I replied.

"No. It's something else," Boom Boy answered.

"The Good Egg washing my dad's car?"

"Would you just come look already?!"

I walked to the front door with Boom Boy. He grabbed the handle and turned it slowly. As he was about to open the door, he looked at me and said, "You might want to step back a little."

"Don't worry," I assured him. "It's not really a tree rat, just a squirrel."

"Suit yourself," he said, and let the door fly open.

The moment he did, a wind stronger than the sucking power of King Justice's vacuum assault on the dirt under the couch wrapped around me. The force caused me to stumble forward, and I fell out the door.

That was when I realized two things.

THING #1

When someone tells you that you may want to take a step back before they open the door, it is most likely due to Thing #2.

THING #2

My house was flying through the sky.

I managed to grab the end of the porch. My feet dangled above the earth — about ten thousand feet above the earth. Wind whipped around my body. My grip slipped.

"Grab my hand!" Boom Boy shouted over the howling winds.

He fell to his knees and extended his arm. Spelling Beatrice rushed to his side and the two pulled me back to safety.

Or at least the safety of a house that was flying ten thousand feet up in the sky.

Spice Girl pressed her face against the window.

"What are you doing?!" Spelling Beatrice barked.

"Looking for the lady on the broom," Spice Girl answered, and scanned the skies. "I can't wait to meet the Munchkins!"

"Do you think we're under attack from the Cloud People?" Exact Change Kid asked.

"If it is them, they'll be sorry when we sidekicks rain on their parade," I answered.

"I thought they rained on our parade, remember? All the *papier mâché* floats got soggy and fell apart. And, none of us actually has rain powers," Exact Change Kid corrected.

"I meant it as a figure of speech."

"Oh. A figure of speech. Well none of us have any figurative rain powers, either."

Spelling Beatrice loaded Scrabble tiles into her utility belt. "Do you really think it's the Cloud People again?"

"I don't know, but who or whatever it is, we better be ready. Were any members of the League of Big Justice in the house?"

Exact Change Kid stepped forward. He thumbed through a notepad. "All the members of the League of Big Justice were given yard duty except for King Justice and Pumpkin Pete."

"Awesome! With King Justice here, we've got nothing to worry about!" I replied. "Where is he?"

"Well, I asked him to clean the cat box, and the last time I saw him he was carrying the kitty litter outside," my mom explained.

"You asked the world's greatest superhero to clean the cat box?" I couldn't believe it.

"Kitty Bumpkins needs a clean place to poo, too." My mom crossed her arms to emphasize her point.

"King Justice? KING JUSTICE? Are you here?" I called out. Nothing. So, while we were hurtling through the atmosphere toward some unknown danger, one that could possibly destroy us and the world, the earth's greatest superhero was scraping Kitty Bumpkins's clumpable poo-litter into a trash can at the curb of my house.

Or at least the curb where my house *used* to be.

"Hey! What happened?" Pumpkin Pete grumbled as he strolled into the living room. "I was watching *Saved by the Bell* and the cable went out!"

"We're off to see the Wizard!" Spice Girl clapped her hands.

"Well, I sure hope the bum's got cable. I have to see how Zack and Screech are gonna get out of that mess!" Pete turned and stomped back toward the TV room.

"Pete! We're under attack!" I called out.

"I should've known! They always cut the cable first!" Pete slammed a viney fist into his palm. "I *hate* evil! It just makes me want to puke!"

"Pete, we have to think of a plan."

"Good idea! A plan . . ." Pete scratched his big, fat orange pumpkin chin. "First, we have to find out where they cut the cable. Did they hit the main cable plant, the place where all cable is born, or is it just an isolated attack on this house? And if it *is* an isolated attack on this house, then I'm outta here! I still got all the channels at my apartment."

"I don't think they're after our cable TV," I suggested. "My house's been torn from the foundation and right now we're flying thousands of feet in the air."

"And when this house was torn from its foundation, did they not also cut your cable TV cable?" Pete questioned.

"Yeah, I guess so . . ."

"Then it would seem that they are indeed after your cable TV!" Pete jabbed a viney finger in my face. "Or do you really expect me to believe all this is just a coincidence?!"

"Pete! The cable was snapped when the house was ripped from the ground!" I growled.

"*Or* . . . was the house ripped from the ground to snap the cable?" Pete jabbed his other finger in my face.

"I think he's on to something," Spice Girl agreed.

The Sidekicks fell into line and Pete paced back and forth like a detective with a pumpkin head. "So, the next question we have to ask ourselves is: 'Who could possibly benefit by cutting off your cable TV?'"

"The Cowardly Lion!" Spice Girl shouted.

"I'll tell you who! Satellite TV, that's who!" Pete spun and faced the Sidekicks. "With cable

TV out of the way, satellite TV can just move in with their little dishes and satellites and suddenly, BLAMMO! They control the greatest power the world knows!"

"The White House?" Exact Change Kid gasped.

"No! Television! This is a battle for Prime Time! For TGI Fridays, Must-See Thursdays, and Whatever-They-Call-It Tuesdays!" Pete shouted. "Yes . . . the bell may have saved us all these years, but now we're the ones who must save the bell!" He headed for the front door.

"Pete! NO!" I shouted.

Pete flung open the front door. He teetered forward on his feet. I raced toward him at 36 miles per hour and tackled him away from the door. We rolled on the floor, and Pete sprang to his feet.

"Okay! Which one of you can fly again?" Pete asked.

A look of terror crossed the Sidekicks' faces.

"Maaa pam!" Boy-in-the-Plastic-Bubble Boy shouted, and everyone ran for cover like cockroaches scampering away from a bright light.

"What? You think I'd just throw one of you out the door to see if you can fly?" Pete huffed. "You! Lady! Can you fly?"

"That's my *mom*!" I reminded Pete.

"And moms can't fly?"

"Not mine."

"Has she ever tried?"

"No."

"No time better than the present!"

Pete took a step toward my mother. She whipped out a spatula and smacked Pete across his pumpkin head. "Don't even think about it, squash-head."

Pete grumbled and stomped toward the couch. Exact Change Kid scrambled out the other side on his hands and knees. "I can't fly! I can't fly!" he squealed repeatedly.

Pete fumed.

"I hate to ask, Pete, but why do you think everyone can fly but me?" I questioned.

"Because I already know you're only good for one thing. And trust me when I say that the day I think complaining can save the world, you'll be the first person I call." Pete scanned the room. "Now where's that kid with the big ears? We can just climb on his back and glide to Earth."

"You've thrown Earlobe Lad off the Sidekick Super Clubhouse two times already! He couldn't fly then and he still can't fly now!" I explained.

"Fly, no. *Glide,* maybe."

"He can't fly or glide, Pete! He has super hearing!"

"Oh, and you just *expect* me to believe a kid with giant ears has super hearing? That boy's a glider, I tell you!" Pete fell to the floor and searched under the couch. "A kid with ears that big can't hide forever!"

As Pete scampered about on the floor, I finally realized something. "Hey," I said as the thought hit me, "has *anyone* seen Earlobe Lad?"

Chapter Nine
The Chapter That Tells You What Happened to Earlobe Lad, Even Though I Didn't Know It at the Time!

"Uh . . . hello?" Earlobe Lad whispered.

He waved his arms to the left, then to the right. He rocked slowly back and forth, but couldn't grab the closest branch that hung just inches from his reach. He twisted and turned, then stopped, realizing that if he fell from that height, it would certainly hurt.

Maybe not his body, but his ears, anyway. There was sure to be a very loud *PLOP!* when he hit the ground.

No, Earlobe Lad wasn't hanging precariously from my roof, soaring thousands of feet above the ground. Nor was he hanging precariously from a window, soaring thousands of feet above the ground. In fact, Earlobe Lad was neither soaring nor thousands of feet above the ground. He was, however, hanging precariously.

At least he had that going for him.

See, as we would later find out, when we were flying toward certain doom, Earlobe Lad was hanging by his Spandexed butt from a tree that stood tall and strong in the parking lot of what was once the home to Donutz Village.

Earlier that day, he had quietly strolled up to Donutz Village to get his daily Cinnabun. The shop was empty and had yet to open, so Earlobe Lad checked his Super Watch of Time-telling and Wristness once, then twice, but before he could check his watch a third time, something very interesting happened.

Completely unknown to Earlobe Lad, at that very moment, across the street from the park, on the other side of the Sidekick Super Clubhouse, deep inside the heart of the League of Big Justice, and despite my protests, Pumpkin Pete pressed the thirteenth button on the mysterious machine and blew up Donutz Village.

The blast sent Earlobe Lad sailing through the air like a Spandex-covered sidekick sailing through the air. Which made sense and all, since he was a Spandex-covered sidekick, and . . . uh . . . he was sailing through the air.

He landed in the tree, a thick, gnarled branch snagging on his Spandex and catching his fall. There he hung and watched as the other sidekicks showed up one-by-one. He had whispered for help as loudly as he could. When that didn't work, he mumbled with all his might, but the only response he received was the response anyone would receive if they hung from the highest branch in a tree and whispered "Help me" to the people down the street.

On a normal day, he would've only had to wait until Exact Change Kid called roll, which was about once an hour. But on this day, Exact Change Kid's usual roll call schedule was interrupted by my mom's arrival in the family station wagon.

Half a day later, Earlobe Lad still hung there like a forgotten, Spandex-wearing piñata with giant ears and thoughts of doughnuts swirling through his head. At least he avoided Pumpkin Pete throwing him out the front door of my house, shouting, "Fly, Earboy! Fly!"

"Hey! Who are you supposed to be? Omelet

Man?" a gruff-looking kid yelled up to Earlobe Lad. "You got egg powers or something?"

"No," Earlobe Lad called back in a low, nearly inaudible voice. "I'm Earlobe Lad. I have super hearing."

"Hey, Omelet Man! Where's Waffle Boy?" A blond kid yelled up to Earlobe Lad.

"I told you, my name is Earlobe Lad!"

"Show us your egg powers!" a third boy laughed.

"I don't *have* egg powers! I have super hearing."

"If you don't have egg powers, then how come you're covered in egg?"

Earlobe Lad thought for a second, then answered, "I'm not covered in —"

An egg splatted on Earlobe Lad's face. The three boys laughed so hard they nearly cried.

"Go get 'em, Omelet Man!" the blond boy shouted, and threw another egg at Earlobe Lad.

The egg cracked across Earlobe Lad's chest. Gooey yolk soaked into his Spandex. "Stop it! Don't you know who I am? I'm a sidekick! I punch evil in the —"

"Egg powers, activate!" the gruff-looking boy yelled. A moment later, a barrage of eggs sailed toward Earlobe Lad and splattered across his body and the tree.

Earlobe Lad swung to the left. He swung to the right. He waved his arms and kicked his feet. He did everything he could to make sure that the three boys laughed even harder every time they hit him with an egg. "Could you at least pummel me with eggs a little more quietly?" Earlobe Lad moaned in a low voice.

"And *this* is for Donutz Village!" the blond boy yelled, and threw his final egg.

As he hung from the branches, egg dripping from his Spandex and face, Earlobe Lad could at least take consolation in one ridiculous fact: Although it was a result of Pumpkin Pete's button-pushing, it cannot be denied that Earlobe Lad blew up before Boom Boy ever did.

"Say hello to Waffle Boy for us, Omelet Man!" the third boy chuckled as the threesome walked away.

"I already told you," Earlobe Lad sighed, exhausted from the onslaught, egg dripping from his face and body, "my name is Earlobe Lad."

Chapter Ten
Mikey's Big Day

After seemingly endless hours of flying, the house finally landed with a booming *THUD!*

"Can I wear the Ruby Slippers first?" Spice Girl asked as she peaked out from behind the couch.

"For the last time, we're not in Oz!" I growled.

Spice Girl ran to the window. "Well, we're not in Kansas anymore, either."

"Where *are* we?" Spelling Beatrice looked at me.

I joined Spice Girl at the window. "I don't think the Cloud People are behind this."

I looked out the window. We were in the middle of a jungle. Vines and trees obscured my view. The air was warm and humid, and I thought I heard the sound of the ocean. We were like castaways, lost on some faraway tropical island, but instead of a boat with a hole in it, we had a flying house with no cable.

"We're doomed!" Pete lamented as he scanned TV station after TV station of static.

No, this wasn't the handiwork of the Cloud People. How could it be? Cloud People live in the clouds. That's why they call themselves "Cloud People." Although, to this day, Spice Girl still thinks that they call themselves "Clown People."

"They're not very funny," Spice Girl had said as the Cloud People flew overhead and blasted downtown in their hovercraft.

"Invasion hordes are *never* funny!" I replied, diving out of the way of falling debris.

"Except for invading hordes of clowns," Spice Girl corrected.

But, as I looked out the window, I knew two things for sure. Clowns, in fact, are not funny, and the Cloud People were not behind the transport of my house.

"Maaph ma pam ma maam? Ma pam pam ma maah phamm," Boy-in-the-Plastic-Bubble Boy said.

"What?" I said.

"Maaph ma pam ma maam? Ma pam pam ma maah phamm," Boy-in-the-Plastic-Bubble Boy repeated.

"I'm sorry, I just don't understand what you're saying."

"MAAPH MA PAM MA MAAM? MA PAM PAM MA MAAH PHAMM!" Boy-in-the-Plastic-Bubble Boy yelled.

"Is it me? Am I the only one who has no idea what the heck he's saying?" I turned to Boy-in-the-Plastic-Bubble Boy's Giant Hamster Ball of Justice. "What are you saying? WHAT?!" I banged on the side of the Hamster Ball of Justice.

"This is no time for jokes," Exact Change Kid cut in. "Boy-in-the-Plastic-Bubble Boy's right. We need to devise a plan and do some recon."

"He did not say that! How the heck do you know he said that?" I blurted.

The Sidekicks stared blankly at me.

"He's about as funny as the Clown People," Spice Girl commented.

"Run! Run! We're under attack!" Pumpkin Pete shouted as he ran into the room. "They're monsters, I tell ya! Monsters!"

Everyone dove for cover. I quickly crawled

over to Pete. "What is it, Pete? Who's attacking us?"

"Is it the flying monkeys?" Spice Girl asked.

Pete's eye darted about in a panic. "Worse! A billion, jillion times worse! It's worse than worse! It's really worse!"

"What is it, Pete? What?!"

"Look!" Pete thrust out a container of canned pumpkin. "I found it in the kitchen pantry!" he gasped. "Soon, they'll be putting all of us in cans! Like cattle!"

I looked at the can. GOOD EATS PUMPKIN PIE FILLING. IF IT'S GOOD EATS, IT EATS GOOD! the label read.

"Pete, my mom bought that at the store," I informed him. "It was for Thanksgiving."

"Gaaah! It's worse than I feared!" Pete howled. "They're making my people into THANKS-GIVING PIES!!!!"

"ATTENTION LEAGUE OF BIG JUSTICE!" a voice boomed over a loudspeaker. "PREPARE TO MEET YOUR DOOM!"

"Aaaaah! They're coming for my head!" Pete shouted. He grabbed his orange skull and raced to the closet. "They want my big, fat, orange pumpkin head for Thanksgiving pie!!!!"

"ATTENTION LEAGUE OF BIG JUSTICE!" the

voice called out again. "PREPARE TO MEET YOUR DOOM!"

"We got it the first time!" Boom Boy yelled out the front door.

"Why do they think we want to meet Doom?" Spice Girl asked.

"They didn't say 'meet Doom,'" I clarified. "They said 'meet your doom.'"

"That's silly," Spice Girl snorted. "I don't even have a doom. And if I did, I certainly wouldn't call him 'doom.' I'd probably call him 'Mr. Skittles.'"

Not that I've ever tried to make sense out of anything Spice Girl has said, or, for that matter, anything Boy-in-the-Plastic-Bubble Boy or Exact Change Kid have ever said, either, but before I could ask what in the world she was talking about, the loudspeaker spoke again.

"Okay, we've given you time to prepare to meet your doom, so, now that you *are* prepared to meet it, it is time for you to . . . uh . . . meet it."

"Would you just shut up and blast them already?!" another voice complained over the loudspeaker.

"Give me back my microphone!" the first voice whined. "We agreed *I* was the one who got to tell the League of Big Justice to prepare to meet their doom! Why are you so mean? If you had a problem with it, you should have said something before!"

"I *did* say something, and you started to cry!" the second voice snapped. "I just went along with this stupid plan to shut you up!"

The bickering voices echoed through the loudspeaker, causing a feedback shriek. As the shrill sound died down, I could hear sniffling.

"Oh, great!" A third voice came over the loudspeaker. "She's crying again! I totally hope you're happy."

"Ha! She always cries!" the second voice said.

"'Cause you're so mean!" the first voice barked. "Can I please finish now?"

There was a moment of silence. Then the first voice cleared her throat. "ATTENTION LEAGUE OF BIG JUSTICE!" the voice boomed. "PREPARE TO MEET YOUR —"

"Skip that part already!" the second voice yelled.

I wasn't about to wait around for our mysterious hosts to decide what doom we should meet and when we should meet it. Besides, meeting doom is bad enough. Meeting doom in my house where it can see embarrassing photos of me, which I know my mom would be all too eager to show, is like meeting doom's doom.

That's just too much doom for one guy to take. Except maybe for Doom Doom Man. He had the power for people to meet *him*. Before he attacked, he would always shout stuff like "Prepare to meet me!" or "You have met your me!" and "Prepare to be covered in gooey maple syrup." I don't think maple syrup has anything to do with doom. I just think he liked to cover people in it.

"We've got to get out of here before they attack," I warned the Sidekicks. "We've got to protect my mom!"

"And me!" Pumpkin Pete cried out from the closet. "I don't want to be a pie!"

"Oh, son! I'm so proud of you!" my mom gushed. "But maybe all these people need is a good talking-to — just someone to sit them down and set them straight."

"And give them a big hug," Spice Girl added.

"No! No hugs and no talking-to! These aren't kids we're talking about! They're evil! They're worse than evil! They're evil with doom to be met! That doom may be a plan, it may be a horde, or it may just be a nasty bulldog with a bad attitude, but it's still doom!" I zipped to the door and grabbed the knob. "Mom! Go hide somewhere!"

"I got dibs on the closet!" Pumpkin Pete yelled out from the closet.

"Once you're safe, the Sidekicks and I will handle whatever waits beyond this door!" I continued. "Now who's with me?"

"Maaa pam mam papm mah mamm! Mam! Mam! MAM! MAM!" Boy-in-the-Plastic-Bubble Boy shouted.

I leaned over to Spelling Beatrice. "Uh . . . is he with me or against me?"

"With you."

"Good."

My palms were sweaty. The doorknob felt like it weighed a thousand pounds. My heart pounded in my chest. "I don't know what dangers wait for us beyond this door. . . . I don't know what evil lurks beyond these walls . . . but one thing I do know is that we're superhero sidekicks! Sworn to protect good! Sworn to right wrongs! Sworn to —"

"Shut up and open the door already!" Boom Boy grumbled. "Always with the speeches, this guy."

I turned the doorknob and flung open the

door, only to be faced with the most terrifying sight the world had ever seen . . .

Teenage girls!

"So, who wants to be destroyed first?" the tall one asked.

Chapter Eleven
Mikey's Summer Vacation

"Allow us to introduce ourselves," the tall girl continued. "We are the Brotherhood of Rotten Babysitters!"

"But you're girls," Boom Boy commented.

"And . . . ?"

"Shouldn't you be a *sisterhood*?"

"I told you!" the thin girl snarled.

"Don't blame me!" the girl with glasses defended. "I voted for 'the Sisterhood of Rotten Babysitters.'"

"The *Sisterhood* of Rotten Babysitters?!" the tall one spat back. "We'd sound like a feel-good movie released in late summer! No one's afraid of feel-good movies!"

"I am," Exact Change Kid confessed. "They always have kissing."

"Trust me, *The Divine Secrets of the Ya-Ya Sisterhood* ruined it for all us evil females," the tall one said.

"I don't care if you're a brotherhood of girls or a sisterhood of guys, I just want to know why you ruined my house and brought us here!" I said.

"I'll bet you'd just love to know the answer to that one." The tall girl crossed her arms. A small smile cut across her face. She stood, silent, defiant, until the girl with glasses asked, "Well, are you going to tell them or what?"

"Look, you *really* have to work on your dramatic tension, Bunni!" the tall one scolded. "I thought we agreed: dramatic tension!"

"*Pfft.* It was more like dramatic boredom," the girl who wasn't Bunni commented, and rolled her eyes. "You were totally standing there with this total 'duh' expression on your face like you didn't even know why we brought them here."

"I know *why* we brought them here! Destroy the League of Big Justice? Hell-loo?! It was, like, *my* idea, Candi," the tall one sneered.

"It was *so* not your idea!" Candi snorted. "You are totally trippin' right now, Kiki."

"Me? Trippin'?! Look in a mirror and check out the poster child for trippin'."

"You're just mad because Brad Jones totally asked *me* to Homecoming instead of you," Candi mocked.

"Brad Jones!? He is *so* last semester!" Kiki snorted. "Hel-lo? I'm a junior now!"

"Uh . . . girls?" I interrupted. "Maybe we could get back to your evil plot and all?"

"STAY OUT OF THIS!" Kiki and Candi shouted at me.

So Kiki was the tallest one. She had black hair and always seemed to be scowling. Candi had blond hair, was thin, and rolled her eyes at a lot. Bunni had red hair, glasses, and liked to smile.

As Kiki and Candi bickered, Boom Boy whispered, "I call dibs on the blond one."

"*I* like the blond one!" Exact Change Kid whispered back.

"I thought you liked brunettes," Boom Boy replied.

"Usually I do. But I figure the blond one looks the nicest and maybe she won't kill me," Exact Change Kid confessed.

"Guys, I really think they're here looking for a fight," I informed them.

"Good! I like feisty girls!" Boom Boy clapped his hands together.

"No. I mean we have to fight them and stop them from destroying the League of Big Justice . . . and us!"

"You're just saying that because you're stuck with the redhead!" Boom Boy sneered.

"Mam pam? Phaam ma ma paa?" Boy-in-the-Plastic-Bubble Boy joined in.

"Okay. You get the redhead. Just stay away from my girl!" Boom Boy warned him. "I really think she might be the one."

"The *one*? The one to crush you under her evil boot heel, you mean!" I answered.

"I don't know, but I've got a fistful of pennies ready just in case," Exact Change Kid said. "I hate rejection."

And, in fact, Exact Change Kid hated rejection so much, the moment that Kiki and Candi finished their argument, Exact Change Kid pelted them with a handful of change.

"Eat copper!" he shouted.

The coins hit the two girls and fell to the ground.

"So . . . if you're free for lunch later, maybe we could . . . I mean . . . unless you're busy or . . . I . . . uh . . ." Exact Change Kid fumbled for words.

Boom Boy dropped his head into his hands. "He is *so* killing our chances."

"Maaa pa!" Boy-in-the-Plastic-Bubble Boy agreed. I think.

Kiki grabbed Exact Change Kid by the collar. "I have dealt with crying kids and dirty diapers. I've had juice spilled on me, SpaghettiOs thrown at me, strained peas flung at me, and gum stuck to me. I've been forced to watch *Finding Nemo* five hundred and thirty-six times and know every single lyric to every single song from every single Disney movie, sequel, prequel, DVD, direct-to-video video, special edition, and stage play. So don't even think for a second that sixty-two pennies bouncing off my face would even make me blink — except for that one that actually hit me in the eye. Your coins can't harm me! I'm made of *steel*! I'm a *babysitter*!"

Exact Change Kid gritted his teeth and leaned closer to Kiki's face. "Don't think I won't use quarters . . ."

"Would everyone just calm down and tell me who the heck you are?!" I shouted.

"And do you like pumpkin pie?" Pete's faint voice called out from the closet.

"So," Kiki began, letting go of Exact Change Kid, "you want to know the origin of the Brotherhood of Rotten Babysitters?"

"Yes!" the word exploded from my mouth.

Chapter Twelve
The Origin of the Brotherhood of Rotten Babysitters!

"We got tired of babysitting all those brats, so we became evil," Kiki explained.

"Rotten," Candi corrected.

"Rotten," Bunni agreed.

Chapter Thirteen
The Revenge of Mikey!

"That's it? *That's* your big 'origin'?!" I sputtered.

"Well, that and the aliens that blasted us with cosmic rays as we drove near the nuclear reactor while eating Pop Rocks and Pepsi and listening to CDs backwards during the lightning storm that happened on the same day as those mysterious sunspots that made the gamma bomb experiment to explode early, causing shards of the green meteor from this dying planet to hit us before we were safely out of Area 51, while watching the Janet Jackson halftime show from the Super Bowl. The next day we had super powers. But that part's *so* five minutes ago," Kiki explained.

"That's my favorite perfume," Spice Girl whispered.

"And now, we've been hired to totally destroy the League of Big Justice!" Candi growled.

"Well, you chicks are out of luck," Boom Boy laughed. "The League of Big Justice is back doing yard work at Speedy's."

"All of them?" Kiki looked like she was about to explode.

"Yes! All of them!" Pete's muffled voice cried out from the closet. "Especially the ones you can make into pies!"

"Who was that?" Kiki demanded.

"Meow! Meow!" Pete replied.

"Why do you want to destroy the League of Big Justice?" I asked.

"*Why?*" Kiki sneered. "We're rotten babysitters! It's just what we do."

"My colleague and I have a question," Exact Change Kid said, looking up from his notebook. He had been scribbling during the whole conversation and also conferring with Spelling Beatrice. He flipped back one page, briefly read his notes, then asked, "Are you 'rotten babysitters' because you're no good at babysitting, or are you babysitters who are rotten, and therefore do bad things? I hope you can see my confusion.

The way you use it, 'rotten' is modifying 'babysitter,' making it sound like an assessment of your babysitting skills rather than a commentary on your moral disposition. While you've been divulging your plan to destroy the League of Big Justice and then rule the world or whatever, I've taken the liberty of sketching out a few alternatives to help avoid any future misunderstandings. So, let me run these by you and maybe you can get some immediate feedback from the other sidekicks." He flipped over two more pages and cleared his throat. The three evil babysitters exchanged unsure looks. "Okay . . . sticking with the babysitting theme . . . how about . . . 'The Brotherhood of Babysitters Who Are Rotten'? or 'The League of Morally Suspect Babysitters'? Oh, here's a good one: 'The Babinators.' Or maybe 'Babysitting Destructo Force-1'? And then there's my personal favorite —"

Before Exact Change Kid could reveal his favorite, Kiki blasted him through the front door.

"Now we'll never know his personal favorite," Spice Girl lamented.

"Sidekicks, attack!" I shouted.

"That's unofficial . . . ," Exact Change Kid moaned from outside, and collapsed into unconsciousness.

I didn't have time to worry whether "Side-kicks, attack!" was our official battle cry or not. I had three crazy babysitters on my hands. If you ask me, all babysitters are evil anyway, but usually the only wicked plot they have the ability to inflict is to ruin your evening of TV or crush your hopes to stay up late. But give a babysitter super powers and you're just asking for trouble.

And that's just what these three were: trouble — with a capital *T*.

I once fought trouble with a little *T*. Actually, it was an evil duo who called themselves Tiny Trouble and Little T.

"I shall trouble your kneecaps!" Tiny Trouble had yelled as he attacked with Little T at his side. "We've got twice the *T* and half the size!"

Unfortunately, Pumpkin Pete had a sneezing fit just as the battle began and ended up inhaling both of them. I think they still live inside his head.

But there would be no inhaling these three.

Candi's hands turned frosty blue and sent a bolt of ice at me, but I was too fast. I zipped out of the way, raced across my living room at 29 miles per hour, and delivered a right cross to her chin.

"Dude! Dude! You hit a girl!" Boom Boy yelled as I skidded to a stop next to him. "And a cute one, too!"

"They're girls second and evil first!" I reminded him.

"Actually, I think they're really bad dressers first, evil second, and girls third," Spice Girl corrected. "And don't *even* get me started on their makeup."

"I don't care how evil or badly dressed they are," Boom Boy argued. "I don't hit girls!"

Boom Boy was suddenly swept off his feet by Bunni's telekinetic powers and slammed against the wall. The dry wall cracked from the impact. Boom Boy let out a pained grunt and fell to the floor.

"Boom Boy!" Spelling Beatrice cried out. She readied four *L* Scrabble tiles in one hand and two *R* tiles in the other.

Boom Boy slowly rose to one knee, his teeth still clenched in pain. "I may not hit girls," he said in an unsteady voice, "but I didn't say anything about not blowing them up!"

Boom Boy leaped into action. Actually, he stood and balled his fists. His cheeks trembled as his face turned red. "Blow you . . . to the . . . moon," he grunted through clenched teeth.

"Maaa pam pam mamama!" Boy-in-the-Plastic-Bubble Boy shouted as he charged his Hamster Ball of Justice toward Kiki.

Spice Girl pulled out all the stops and launched a curry-and-black-pepper attack, causing Candi to sneeze like a giant runny nose in a hay fever factory.

Candi retaliated by shooting deadly icicles from her hands. They rocketed across the living room and sliced up Spice Girl's Spandex outfit like a wasabi-crazed chef in an all-you-can eat sushi bar.

"Ooo! I just got this back from the dry cleaners!" Spice Girl shouted, and let loose with cilantro and paprika. "Smell *this*!"

Boy-in-the-Plastic-Bubble Boy's Giant Hamster Ball of Justice Bowling Ball Blitzkrieg on Kiki ended abruptly when Bunni used her telekinetic powers to bounce him between the floor and the ceiling like a giant, human Ping-Pong ball. "Ma — Pam — Mam — Pa — Ma — Mmm!" he shouted and half-grunted with each impact.

Spelling Beatrice hurled her *L* tiles. They hit Bunni and let out an electrical shock, breaking her concentration. The Hamster Ball of Justice fell to the ground, but it was too late. Boy-in-the-Plastic-Bubble Boy slid down the concave side of his hamster ball. "Maaaaa . . . ," he groaned as he fell unconscious.

The next thing I knew, Candi had encased Boom Boy in an ice block and Spelling Beatrice, Spice Girl, and I were on the run.

"Hide under the bed! Hide in the closet! Hide behind the couch! It won't matter! No one can hide from a babysitter!" Kiki shouted at us as we raced out the front door. "Especially an *evil* babysitter!"

"Rotten," Candi corrected.

"Rotten," Bunni agreed.

Chapter Fourteen
Mikey and the Case of the Swiped Sweets!

I didn't want to run. I'd never run from a fight before. I once ran away from this girl who asked me to the movies, but that was only because I kept stuttering when I tried to answer her. I figured it was less embarrassing to yell "Look out!" and run in the opposite direction than it was to continue to stand there stammering.

I was wrong about that one. For the next six months, every time her friends saw me at school, they'd yell "Look out!" and run in the opposite direction.

But today I ran. We needed to regroup, and

more importantly, I needed to get the Rotten Babysitters away from my house and my mom's hiding place.

"Now what?" I asked Spelling Beatrice and Spice Girl.

We seemed to be on some island and, despite Spice Girl's insistence, there was neither a Yellow Brick Road nor flying monkeys.

"But when we find them, I know one kid who can blow up who'll owe me an apology!" Spice Girl warned.

"I can't blow up. I have super speed," I reminded her.

"Then why do you call yourself 'Le Poop'?" she asked.

"Do you think they were the ones who sent the machine with all the buttons?" Spelling Beatrice asked.

"I dunno," I began. "It seems odd. If they were powerful enough to rip my house from its foundation and fly us here, why send us a machine with buttons?"

"So, two *different* groups want to kill the League of Big Justice," Spelling Beatrice said in realization.

That's one thing I never understood about supervillains. These people spend a lot of time planning, plotting, thinking, trying, and hoping to destroy the League of Big Justice. I mean, it's really, really unhealthy behavior. Do they get up and check their calendar and it says *WEDNES-DAY: DESTROY LEAGUE OF BIG JUSTICE, or TUESDAY: TRY TO RULE THE WORLD?* So they get dressed, go out, and try to destroy the League of Big Justice. It's like, "So, what're you doing today?" "Oh, just planning to destroy the League of Big Justice." "Really? I was plotting to destroy them, too."

I mean, come on! Get a life! Or at least a hobby. (A hobby besides trying to destroy the League of Big Justice, I mean.) Between all the planning, plotting, and attacking, they really don't have much time to just sit back and enjoy the little things in life.

No wonder they're supervillains.

The three of us took refuge in the jungle island's thick underbrush. "We have to think of a plan," I said.

"Well, you could bring the punch and cookies, and Spelling Beatrice can bring party games, and I can bake a nice cake with sprinkles on top," Spice Girl said brightly.

"I mean a plan to defeat the Brotherhood of Rotten Babysitters," I clarified.

"Yeah, I know," she said and rolled her eyes. "That's my plan."

"How can we defeat them with cake and party games?"

"I'm glad you asked. While I serve the punch, you pull out the Twister board and we —"

"It was a rhetorical question," I snapped.

"Oh. Sorry. I'm bad at math." Spice Girl scratched her head as the bright smile left her face.

"SIDEKICKS!" Kiki's voice boomed over the same loudspeaker we had heard before. "We know you're out there! No one can escape . . . Skull Island!"

"Skull Island?" Spice Girl repeated. "What an icky name."

"What do you want?!" I called back.

The only answer I received was a shower of icicle spears from Candi. We couldn't see them, and I knew they couldn't see us. The deadly attack was sent in the direction of my voice. We dove for cover and barely prevented the sharp tips of the ice missiles from turning us into Spandex shish kebabs.

"They're more powerful than we are!" Spelling Beatrice said. "I could run circles around them on the SATs, but . . ." she looked around at the dense jungle, "I'm a little out of my element here. If I'd only brought my thesaurus!"

"We need to find a classroom!" Spice Girl suggested.

"No. We have to find the Rotten Babysitters' weakness. Aw! Where's Super Vision Lad when you really need him?" I complained. "Come on, think! What's every babysitter's weakness?"

"Parents who don't pay!" Spice Girl said.

"No . . . something else . . ."

"Parents who don't tip!" she said.

"No! It's not parents!" I saw Spice Girl's face brighten. "And it's not cold pizza, either!"

Her smile disappeared again and her shoulders drooped. "Well, it could be," she mumbled.

"I think we have to take out Bunni first. She's the most dangerous," Spelling Beatrice suggested.

"Any ideas?" I asked.

"With those telekinetic powers, she can nullify my tiles and your speed . . ."

"My speed? How?"

"It's hard to run one hundred miles per hour when you're floating upside down," Spelling Beatrice reminded me.

"Oh, yeah. *That.*"

"So, I was thinking," Spelling Beatrice went

on, "and hear me out before you just say 'no.' I was thinking, the only powers she can't stop are . . ."

She didn't say it. She didn't need to say it. I already knew the answer.

"Why is everyone staring at me?" Spice Girl asked. Her eyes widened and she quickly lifted her hand to shield her face. "Is there a booger in my nose?"

"Bunni's telekinetic powers can't stop your . . . smell." As each word left my mouth, it sounded more and more insane. That's probably because it *was* insane and becoming more and more so with each word that left my mouth. "*You* have to stop Bunni."

Spice Girl thought about this for a moment, then asked, "Do you mean 'stop' as in 'Stop in the Name of Love' or 'Stop' as in *Stop! Or My Mom Will Shoot*? I sure hope it's not *that* one, because it was a really stupid movie with that guy who yelled 'Adrian!' all the time in that other movie where he punched stuff. I think that movie was called *The Man Who Punched Stuff.*"

I looked at Spelling Beatrice. "What's your *other* idea?"

"Sidekicks!" Kiki's voice blared again. "We have a little surprise for you!"

The moment we heard Kiki, we hunkered down, hiding beneath the leaves and brush. None of us were going to answer this time and let them get a bead on our location.

The time seemed to stretch into minutes and the silence chewed at me like a tree rat.

"Well, are you gonna tell them the surprise, or what?" we heard Bunni ask.

"What did we just talk about not *five minutes* ago?" Kiki spat back.

"Getting pedicures every Sunday once we rule the world?" Bunni replied.

"No! *Dramatic tension*!" Kiki yelled.

"I totally think you don't even know what dramatic tension is," Candi joined in. "Because every time you say you're creating dramatic tension, you're just totally standing there like . . . 'Duh!'"

"It is *not* 'DUH!'" Kiki shouted. "It's the use of silence and inactivity to increase the sense of anxiety between us and them. Come on! It's in the first chapter of the Supervillain Handbook!"

"I thought the first chapter was 'Pompous Speeches, Convoluted Schemes, and Slow-Moving Death Traps,'" Candi stated.

"That's Chapter Six," Kiki corrected. "You didn't even *read* the book, did you?"

"I tried! But that McKenneson brat kept throwing broccoli at me!"

"Uh . . . girls?" I interrupted from my hiding place. "Maybe we could get back to your evil surprise?"

"STAY OUT OF THIS!" Kiki and Candi shouted at me.

"You're just mad that *I* made head cheerleader and you didn't!" Kiki continued.

"Why do I care about being head cheerleader?!" Candi spat back. "I'm totally gonna be ruler of the world!"

"Yeah, but *I'm* gonna be ruler of the world *and* head cheerleader!" Kiki boasted.

"Oh . . . shut up!" Candi fumed.

"You shut up more!" Kiki countered.

"Fine!"

"Fine!"

There was a moment of silence, and then Kiki said, "Okay, sidekicks! Surrender now . . . or else!"

"Speedy!" I heard a weak voice cry out from above me. "Don't listen to them!"

The voice sounded too familiar, and then I finally saw them. They were above us, standing on a hover platform. My mom was with them.

The Brotherhood of Rotten Babysitters had my mom.

It was time to kick some babysitter butts. "No more messing around. We take them out. Now."

"But Boom Boy already had dibs on the blond girl," Spice Girl reminded me.

"I don't mean take them out on a date. I mean take them out of commission!" I had never been more serious in my life. My mom was in trouble, and even worse, she was being threatened by babysitters. "Evil babysitters," I said aloud.

"Rotten," Spelling Beatrice corrected.

"Rotten," Spice Girl agreed.

"I'll give you ten seconds to give yourselves up!" Kiki called out. "Or she gets it!"

"Is that, like, ten *real* seconds, or ten 'dramatic tension' seconds?" Candi snorted.

"Would you shut up already?!" Kiki demanded.

"You're just mad because I was, like, voted Most Popular during senior year and you still had braces," Candi said.

"If you were so popular then how come *I* was the only one who signed your yearbook?" Kiki asked.

"That was totally my second yearbook. My first one was already full, Tractor Teeth!"

"Don't call me that!" Kiki shouted.

"Tractor Teeth!" Candi yelled.

"Don't call me that!" Kiki repeated.

"Tuh . . . tuh . . . tuh . . . Tractor Teeth!" Candi mocked.

Bunni started to cry.

"Why are you crying now?" Kiki demanded.

"I hate it when you two fight," Bunni sniffed. "We're supposed to be rotten babysitters, but I think we're just rotten friends . . ."

Kiki and Candi looked at each other, and then broke out in apologies, tears, and hugs.

"I'm sorry!" Candi sniffed.

"No! I'm sorry," Kiki added. "Come on, let's destroy the Sidekicks and rule the world."

"You'd still want to rule it with me?" Candi asked, wiping away a tear.

Kiki held up a charm bracelet on her wrist. It was one-third of a whole. Candi and Bunni held up their thirds. I couldn't see what it said, but somehow I knew that when all three were placed together, it said something like "Best Friends: 2 Good 2 B 4-Got-10" and had a picture of a dolphin or a unicorn or something.

These girls *had* to be stopped!

I didn't have much time. My mom was in

their hands and desperate babysitters do desperate things: like microwave macaroni and cheese for dinner. "Spelling Beatrice! You take care of Candi. I'll take care of Kiki and my mom." I turned to Spice Girl. "I'll get Bunni off that platform, then she's all yours. We're counting on you."

"Good," Spice Girl nodded. "But I don't want to count on you. I'm bad at numbers."

We'd get only one chance. If I missed, or Spelling Beatrice couldn't stop Candi, it was going to be a very short fight. At least if Spelling Beatrice or I failed, I wouldn't have to worry about Spice Girl stopping Bunni — which sounded impossibly insane.

I raced toward a tree as fast as I could. Using my super speed, I jumped fifteen feet high to the bottom branch and ricocheted off like a bullet.

Luckily, the hover platform was low enough and my attack sudden enough that I took the Brotherhood of Rotten Babysitters by surprise. I body-slammed Bunni and she fell into the jungle below.

"You stupid little brat!" Candi growled. "No TV for you!"

She raised her hands and was about to freeze

me when Spelling Beatrice's Scrabble tiles sailed through the air, spraying a gooey substance that encased Candi in a glob of goodness. She was immobile and powerless.

"Give it up," I said to Kiki.

"Oooo! If you ever have kids, I'm charging you double-time!" Kiki sneered.

She unleashed a shock blast from her hands, but I was too quick and zipped to the side.

"You move fast, kid. But let's see how fast the old lady moves!"

"Who are you calling 'old'?!" my mom snapped back.

Kiki aimed her hands at my mother. A wicked smile crossed Kiki's face. There wasn't a second to lose! I lunged at Kiki and grabbed her wrists. Both hands twisted upward and the blast shot harmlessly into the sky.

We struggled. Kiki twisted her wrist in my hand and let loose another blast. It barely missed my head. I used all my strength and tried to face her hands upward again. *That* was when she kicked my shin.

Kicking a shin isn't much in a battle between the forces of good and evil with the fate of something important hanging in the balance, but, dang, it hurt! She used the opportunity to break one hand free from my grip. She quickly aimed it at me.

"Bye-bye!" she laughed, and prepared to blast me.

That was when I pushed her off the platform.

Chapter Fifteen
Bananas Taste Good!

Kiki unleashed a series of quick blasts. I dove off the platform after her, and once I hit the ground I was able to use my super speed again. I zigged at 51 miles per hour and zagged at 36 miles per hour. Kiki yelled. Kiki shouted. Kiki had a tantrum.

But Kiki couldn't hit me.

Too bad Kiki couldn't say the same thing.

I raced directly at her, weaving through her power blasts, and delivered a roundhouse, knocking her to the ground.

"I can't believe you hit girls!" Kiki gasped, down on all fours.

"You're no girl. You're a babysitter!" I snarled.

I don't know what that means, but it just sounded like the right thing to say.

Kiki let go another blast. It missed me, but then, she wasn't aiming at me. It hit the trunk of the tree behind me. Kiki rolled to safety and I barely managed to avoid the collapsing branches.

Suddenly, dozens of quick blasts shot out from the jungle. I zigzagged as quickly as I could to avoid Kiki's energy powers. As I sped closer, it became easier for her to hit me. I had to keep running. I had to keep moving. One false step and all would be lost.

Kiki let out a huge blast as I leaped at her. It skimmed my shoulder. The pain felt like dislocation, but I couldn't be stopped. I tackled Kiki and pulled her to the ground. She raised both her hands and prepared to hit me point-blank.

This was gonna hurt. A lot.

Spelling Beatrice jumped out from the jungle, more Scrabble tiles at the ready. She hurled two *S* tiles. "Onomatopoeia!" she shouted as the tiles did their work and encased Kiki in a binding net.

"Come on! We have to help Spice Girl with Bunni!"

I grabbed my aching shoulder as the two of us raced in the direction where Bunni had fallen. Soon we smelled chamomile and cinnamon.

"Uh-oh," I said, "that doesn't smell like a battle."

Spelling Beatrice and I quickened our pace. We raced into a clearing and found . . . well, I'm not exactly sure *what* we found.

"And then . . . and then, after my parents got a divorce, my mom had to work two jobs and I never got to see her." Bunni sniffed. "I didn't really *want* to steal those things from the store . . . I just wanted her attention . . ."

Spice Girl embraced Bunni and patted her on the back. "There, there. It's okay," she assured Bunni. "It's not your fault."

As Bunni cried, Spice Girl looked up and noticed our arrival. "See," Spice Girl said with a warm smile on her face. "Sometimes evil just needs a hug."

I raced back to where we left Kiki. Even though the battle was done, there were still too many questions to be answered. Kiki had mentioned that they were "hired" to destroy the League of Big Justice. I intended to learn who was signing their paychecks.

Or maybe *what* was signing their paychecks. You can never be too sure with supervillains.

"So, you think you've won?" Kiki mocked the moment I raced up.

"Well, if by 'won' you mean that I kicked your butt and we defeated your Brotherhood of Rotten Babysitters — if *that's* what you mean by 'won,' then yeah, I think so."

"Think again," Kiki said. I finally noticed she had wriggled a hand down to her waist. Before I could act, she pushed a button on her belt.

"Okay, is that calling for more babysitters?" I asked.

I heard a loud rumble behind me. A large missile rose slowly from the jungle terrain.

"There's not a chance that's just filled with popcorn, is there?"

"That, my stinking little sidekick, is the Babytron Bomb!" Kiki laughed.

"The Babytron Bomb?!" I gasped. "Wait. What's a Babytron Bomb?"

"When that hits California, the entire Western seaboard will be turned into babies!"

"I thought you hated kids!"

"I DO! But it pays cash, and you can make your own hours. Besides, I've invested all my babysitter and supervillain earnings into stock in diaper companies!" Kiki squirmed in her net, but she wasn't going anywhere. "You may have won the fight, sidekick, but I won the bigger fight! And the next fight will be for cribs and pacifiers!"

"You're insidious!" I yelled.

"No, I'm *rotten*," she corrected.

I pulled out my sidekick Super Wrist Communicator of Tiny Screenness. "Spelling Beatrice! We've got trouble!"

"I know! Is that a missile?!" her tiny face appeared on the tiny screen on my tiny wrist communicator.

"Worse. A Babytron Bomb."

"Oh no! Not a Babytron Bomb!" She gasped. "Wait. What's a Babytron Bomb?"

"No time to explain! I've gotta get up there quick or half the U.S. will be wearing poopy diapers and crying for their mommies!"

"They're despicable!" Spelling Beatrice said.

"ROTTEN! We're *rotten*! Why is that so hard to remember?!" Kiki shouted.

"Why hasn't it blasted off yet?" Spelling Beatrice asked.

I looked to Kiki. She averted her eyes.

"Well?" I asked.

"I . . . uh . . . I like, kind of figured we'd have you captured already when we launched it, so I . . . like . . . kinda extended the countdown time to uh . . . you know . . . give it more . . . you know . . . ," she stammered.

I looked at Spelling Beatrice on my Super Wrist Communicator of Tiny Screenness. "Dramatic tension," I said.

Chapter Sixteen
Bye-Bye, Baby!

The Babytron Bomb rumbled as it slowly lifted off from Skull Island.

It had taken only a few seconds for my mom to navigate the hover platform to the ground. "I'd just like to tell everyone that I am *so* proud of my son!" She showered me with kisses and hugs.

"Mom! Please! You're embarrassing me in front of the supervillains!"

"A loser like you defeated us, and, like, you think *you're* embarrassed?" Candi complained with an eye roll.

And now, there I was, zooming over the jungle. I pressed the throttle lever on the hover platform as hard as I could, hoping to get to the Babytron Bomb before it shot into the sky.

Who knows what I would do once I did get there.

I didn't have much time. I didn't know if I would be coming back. I had so many questions; so many questions that might never be answered. Important questions like, "Why do they call it 'Skull Island' if it's got nothing to do with babysitting and there's not a rock or a mountain that even vaguely looks like a skull?" and "Why couldn't they have used their babysitting powers for good instead of evil?" and perhaps the most important, "Is there *really* a Supervillain Handbook?"

The Babytron Bomb picked up speed. I didn't know how fast the hover platform could fly, I just knew it could never keep up with a Babytron Bomb. I mean, I assume they're fast.

I'd have only one chance. But I couldn't think about that now. I could think only about all those crying babies and stinky diapers. I was the last hope of the Western United States. I was the only thing that stood between salvation and millions of people having to live through puberty a second time. I had to stop the Babytron Bomb even if it meant sacrificing myself.

Some people call it courage. Others, bravery. I call it sheer stupidity.

The thunderous rumbling of the Babytron Bomb filled my ears as it cleared the silo. I dropped the hover platform into overdrive and rammed into the Babytron Bomb's guidance fin at full speed. The impact sent a hard shudder through the hover platform. Its circuits shorted. Sparks and smoke gushed from the split metal, and a second later, the hover platform exploded.

As I fell back to Earth, the last thing I saw before I blacked out was the Babytron Bomb lifting into the sky, a bent fin on its side and a plume of black smoke trailing behind.

I opened my eyes.

I remembered plummeting from the sky. You'd think, falling from that height, I'd have been little more than pudding right now. Although, I still might have been pudding, just with eyes. I lifted my one arm, then the other. Okay, maybe I was pudding with eyes and two arms.

I sat up in bed. I was in my bed, in my room. Spelling Beatrice, Boom Boy, and Boy-in-the-Plastic-Bubble Boy sat next to my bed. Exact Change Kid leaned in through the window.

"I had the strangest dream," I said slowly. "You were there . . . and you, and you, and you!" I continued, pointing to each sidekick.

"It wasn't a dream, Speedy," Spelling Beatrice informed me.

"But . . . then . . . I fell hundreds of feet! I should be pudding!"

"Bunni used her telekinetic powers and lowered you like a feather," Spelling Beatrice explained.

"*Bunni* saved me?!"

"It's amazing what a hug can do," Exact Change Kid added. "We can fly. We can shoot rays from our eyes. We can bend steel bars with our bare hands. We have the powers to crush worlds and topple governments — well, none of *us* can do those things, really, but sort of — and yet none of us have ever stopped to think that maybe there's no power greater than love."

Boom Boy slammed the window down on him.

"Where is Bunni? I mean, I should thank her," I said.

Boom Boy stabbed a thumb toward the living room. "She's sharing eye shadow secrets with Spice Girl."

"And my mom?"

"Right here." I heard her voice as she entered the room. "We're all so proud of you!" she bent over and gave me a kiss on the forehead.

"Mom!" I grumbled, turning red.

I had a million questions. "Do we know who hired the Brotherhood of Rotten Babysitters?"

"Even Bunni says they don't know. It was all done through scrambled messages," Spelling Beatrice said.

"So this isn't over yet. The real enemy is still out there. Maybe with babysitters even more rotten than these. . . ." The thought left me uneasy.

My mom ushered the Sidekicks from the room. "Now all of you run along and let my boy sleep. There'll be plenty of time to discuss evil's secret plan for world domination when he's feeling a little better."

"Wait! What about the Babytron Bomb? Did I stop it?" I called to them.

Spelling Beatrice stopped in the doorway. "Well, I wouldn't say it 'stop' exactly. . . ."

"Where did it land?"

"Paris!" Pumpkin Pete stated as he stepped from my closet.

"Oh no! I turned the city of Paris into whining, crying babies?"

"Eh, it's just the French." Pumpkin Pete shrugged. "You ask me, no one will know the difference."

And the funny thing? He was right. No one did.

Chapter Seventeen
Evil Has a Tantrum

"What are they doing now?" the voice asked.

"Trying to reattach the cable to the house," the minion replied.

"Cable?"

"Yes. Cable."

"I see."

The room was cast in darkness. Long shadows fell across the mysterious figure shrouding his face and body in a gloomy veil. There was a moment of silence while the voice considered the possibilities.

"What kind of cable?" the voice finally asked.

"Cable TV cable."

"I see."

Again, silence. The voice had not foreseen this eventuality. There was a reason. There must be. If only the voice could crack the enigma of this event.

"Don't they have satellite TV? I thought everyone had satellite?" the voice finally asked.

"No, great leader, they still have cable."

"I see."

Possibilities, endless possibilities unfolded like an onion smashed against a wall.

"Do they at least have the premium channels?" the voice asked.

"By our records, they have Bravo and Cinemax, but not HBO," the minion revealed.

"No HBO?! How do they watch *The Sopranos*?"

"The one with the orange pumpkin for a head asked the same thing."

"And the Brotherhood of Rotten Babysitters . . . did they destroy anyone?" the voice asked.

"Counting the cable?" the minion replied.

"No! Not counting the cable!"

"Then no. They destroyed no one. Although Bunni did get a date with Boom Boy."

"A date to *destroy* Boom Boy?" the voice asked hopefully.

"No. A date to Waterslide World. See, apparcntly Bunni didn't get enough hugs as a child and when Spice Girl —"

"Please. I just . . . don't want to know," the voice sighed. "Do we have any more rotten baby-sitters?"

"'Rotten' as in babysitters who lack the skills to properly supervise a child, or are you making a commentary on their moral disposition?"

"I don't care which one! I need someone to destroy the League of Big Justice!" the voice shouted.

The minion accessed his PDA. "Sorry, great leader, but all the remaining contacts we have are merely babysitters who lack the skills to properly supervise a child, such as Mrs. Duck-worth."

"But does she have any super powers? Can she blow things up or blast things? Tell me she at least has the power to blast things!"

"No. But she does have a peculiar odor . . . not unlike mothballs."

There was silence; a long deep silence that set upon the dark room while the voice thought for a moment, considering the multitude of options like a master studying a chessboard.

"And, sir? There's still a matter of payment," the minion reminded him.

"Payment?"

"Yes. We owe each member of the Brotherhood of Rotten Babysitters ten dollars an hour, plus double for every hour they tried to destroy the League of Big Justice after midnight."

"Fine. Fine. Fine. But send it to them in pennies."

"Pennies, O great leader?"

"Yes! Pennies! I *am* evil, you know!"

"Yes, great leader! Of course, great leader!" the minion gushed as he bowed repeatedly and backed out of the room.

"So . . . it would seem I have shown an error in judgment, sending well-dressed teenage girls to destroy the greatest superheroes the world has ever known," the voice said to itself. "No matter. There shall be no mistake next time . . . for I shall destroy the League of Big Justice myself!"

"Uh . . . were you talking to me?" the minion called out from the other room.

"No! I was scheming! Can't I scheme to myself anymore?!" the voice shouted back from the dark room.

The minion did not answer. The voice fumed.

"And another thing!" the voice shouted to the minion. "Get someone to fix this light! I'm tired of sitting in the dark!"

Chapter Eighteen
Charisma Kid Saves the Day!

CHARISMA KID SAVES THE DAY! the newspaper headline screamed. Below it was a picture of the defeated Brotherhood of Rotten Babysitters.

"What?!" I shouted. "Charisma Kid wasn't even there!"

Below that article was another photo of Captain Haggis being cut free from the undergrowth in my backyard by the local fire department. EVIL BUSHES ATTACK WORLD'S GREATEST HEROES! a smaller headline read.

I took off my goggles and threw them across the parking lot. They hit Pumpkin Pete in the head and draped across his face. "Hey, look!" Pete called out. "Free goggles!"

"I quit!" I shouted, as if throwing my goggles wasn't evidence enough.

"You can't quit!" Pete yelled, stomping up to me.

"And why not?!" I huffed.

"Because you're fired!" Pete snarled.

"Then give me back my goggles!"

Pete froze. The goggles' elastic band was stretched to its breaking point as Pete forced them over his head. "So that's how it's gonna be? Well, then, you're *un*fired!" Pete patted me on the back. "But can I keep the goggles?"

"Go ahead," I sighed.

Pete ran off, as excited as a monkey in a banana store. He raced into the League of Big Justice and closed the door behind him. There was a moment of silence; then he cracked open the door again and poked out his head.

"You're fired!" he shouted, then slammed the door.

"Fine," I griped, then turned and walked straight into The Strike.

"You're quitting?" he asked. I don't know who was more surprised, The Strike because I quit, or me because he appeared out of nowhere.

"You're a little late for saving me," I complained.

"I didn't need to save you. You beat those babysitters on your own," The Strike consoled me.

"Wow. Good for me. I beat evil teenage girls."

"And saved your mom and The Sidekicks," The Strike added. "It might be best if you wait until you *lose* a fight before you quit."

"I almost *did* lose this fight. But I'm sure *you* would've saved me. Just like you did with Dr. Robot and the Mole Master, Master of Moles." I crossed my arms. "Now that I think about it, most of the fights I *did* win were only because you saved me."

"But you still won."

"It doesn't matter. Pete fired me," I explained.

"And tomorrow he'll be looking for you at two o'clock!" The Strike laughed.

"Look, you're not one to make big speeches about quitting," I told him. "Didn't you walk out on King Justice twelve years ago?"

"I had a good reason."

"Well, so do I!" I defended. "I'm tired of doing all the work and everyone else getting the credit. I save the world and Pete gets the credit. I save Charisma Kid, and somehow Charisma Kid gets the credit. How do you get the credit for saving your own life?!"

"I can't believe they get *all* the credit," he said.

"Extra! Extra! Read all about it," a young street urchin yelled from the corner, waving a fresh copy of the evening paper in the air. "Charisma Kid saves the world from rotten babysitters!"

I cocked an eyebrow at The Strike.

Suddenly, his utility belt flashed. He pulled out a small communicator. "This warns me when important news breaks!" he explained. The screen came to life.

"We're here with the brave soul who single-handedly fought back the attacking babysitters!" a news reporter barked.

Charisma Kid's pretty mug filled the screen.

"Thank you! Thank you!" he began. "The odds were against me, and even though I wasn't actually on the island where they were defeated and never even fought them, I'm just glad to have done my part to defeat those evil babysitters —"

"Rotten," the news reporter corrected.

"Rotten," the cameraman agreed.

"Yes, yes," Charisma Kid continued. "But this was one battle that I could not have fought alone. There's one sidekick who helped me more than I can say, whose bravery and steely nerve gave me the inspiration to fight against insurmountable odds!"

I perked up. Was he talking about me? He had to be talking about me! There was no one else *to* talk about! I couldn't believe it! It was amazing! It was . . . it was the greatest feeling I had ever —

"Blind-as-a-Bat Boy! I just want the world to hear me say . . . thanks!" Charisma Kid smiled.

Blind-as-a-Bat Boy stuck his head into the corner of the TV screen. "Skree! Skree!" he shrieked.

"You should have seen him batify those babysitters," Charisma Kid bragged.

"Skree!"

"You bet, buddy!" Charisma Kid patted him on the back.

"Skree!"

"Blind-as-a-Bat Boy!? Who the heck is Blind-as-a-Bat Boy!?" I shouted to The Strike.

"You can't quit, Speedy," he said in response.

"Give me one reason," I said.

"Because you're good. And right now, maybe more than ever before, the world needs a hero."

"If the world needs a hero, it can have you again. Besides, I'm sure you'd rather be saving Charisma Kid than me."

"No, I wouldn't. Charisma Kid is a jerk," The Strike said.

He thinks Charisma Kid is a jerk? I could really get to like this Strike guy. But I wasn't convinced that easily.

"Like I said, you're not one to go around telling people to not be quitters. Besides, I have a wonderful future ahead of me as junior assistant florist. Maybe my dad will finally be proud of me then."

"He *is* proud of you, Speedy," The Strike replied immediately.

I stopped and turned around. "How do you know that?"

The Strike looked at the ground. He took a deep breath. I could tell he was struggling with something.

"Well?" I pressed.

"I loved being a superhero," he began. "I used to soar above this city like a bird! Imagine that, Speedy! Imagine the freedom and the joy! I bet it's how you feel when you run — when you don't give a darn about anything and just run!"

"Maybe," I replied without looking at him.

"I knew I'd *never* find something that I loved more than being a superhero."

"If you loved it so much, how come you quit?"

"Because I was wrong. I gave it all up because I *did* find something I loved even more," The Strike explained.

"*Pfff.* What was *that*? Knitting?" I asked, rolling my eyes.

"No. *You.*"

The Strike raised his hands. He slid his fingers under his mask, and what happened next was so mind-boggling, it deserves its own chapter.

Chapter Nineteen
What Happened Next That Was So Mind-Boggling, It Deserves Its Own Chapter!

"DAD?!"

Chapter Twenty
Actually, It Was So Mind-Boggling, It Deserves Two Chapters!

"DAD?!"

Chapter Twenty-one

"Dad?! What're you doing in The Strike's uniform?!" I gasped.

"Son, I *am* The Strike," my dad confessed.

I stared at him for endless seconds, eyes wide, mouth open.

"Dad?! What're you doing in The Strike's uniform?!" I gasped.

My dad smiled. "Haven't you ever wondered how you got your super powers? I mean, usually they're . . . inherited. . . ."

And then it hit me.

"Ohhh, nonononono. No. No. No."

"Guy, I —" my dad began

"No. Nonono. No. It's . . . it's just not possible!

You . . . you couldn't be! You're an accountant! You're . . . you're . . . you're my *dad*!"

"And I've never been more proud to be your dad since you joined The Sidekicks."

My dad was proud of me? Somehow things didn't seem so bad after hearing that.

I wondered aloud. "Why tell me all this now?"

"Because I want you to be happy, son. So does your mother. That's all we've ever wanted for you. Our family was placed in danger today, and I just thought it was time I told you the truth," my dad explained. "We're proud of you, son. Both of us. Now, you don't *need* to stay with The Sidekicks, but . . ."

"Yeah. The world needs a hero. I'll think about it," I said with a sigh.

All this was too much for one kid to absorb. But I did have one question, one that had been burning in my brain since I discovered its existence.

"Dad? Can I ask you something?"

My dad put his mask back on. He grabbed me around the waist and the two of us sailed into the air.

"Shoot."

"Why'd you leave King Justice with that grocery list? I mean, he was your sidekick and all. It's been driving him nuts for twelve years!"

A pained expression came over my dad's face. "I'd thought I left him a letter explaining I was having a son and I was quitting. I didn't realize the mistake until I dusted off the old costume to start watching over you and found the real letter still stashed in the utility belt. I felt terrible!"

"I can give him the real one, if you'd like . . ."

"I *would* like that, son. But maybe King Justice would like it better if it came from me."

Then a funny thought hit me. How did my mom and dad *really* meet? What if . . . what if . . . no way. *That* would be too freaky!

"Dad? Um . . . Mom . . . Mom's not, like, a supervillain, is she?"

He chuckled. "Only if she finds out you forged her signature to play football."

We soared into the moonlit night, superhero and sidekick . . . father and son. And suddenly, things didn't seem so terrible after all.

"Oh, and Guy?" my dad said. "Let's not tell your mom about any of this."

The moon hung high in the night sky. A chill rose in the air, a stinging reminder that winter lurked on the horizon. Dead leaves danced along the ground, pushed ever forward by the icy fingers of the night wind.

A brown owl swooped from the darkness toward an oak tree. It forcefully flapped its wings once, twice, then extended its talons to rest on a high branch of the timeless sentinel.

The owl scanned the terrain below for an unwary mouse, but on this night, the world lay silent, its secrets kept like the cold earth beyond a cemetery's walls.

The owl snapped to attention. Something

moved behind him. A sudden cracking noise from the strained limb of the oak sent the owl airborne. It beat its wings with a certain urgency and quickly disappeared into the cover of night, safe from whatever unseen danger lurked in the branches of the great oak.

"Hello?" Earlobe Lad whispered, still hanging from a thick branch by his Spandex. "Anybody?"

The End

Author Bios
Biographies of the Authors!

Dan Danko attributes his love of comic books to his childhood belief that he's from another planet. To this day, he has yet to be proven wrong.

Dan lists one of his greatest accomplishments as being fluent enough in Japancsc to spcak to a dim-witted seven-year-old. If Dan isn't watching Lakers' games, you'll find him traveling to any country that has a traveler's advisory from the U.S. State Department — much to his mother's dismay.

He's the tall one.

Tom Mason's love of comic books and all things super-heroey began when he had the flu and his parents bought him a stack of comics and scnt him to the doctor.

When he's not selling his family's heirlooms on eBay or scuba diving off the California coast, he enjoys playing horseshoes with a long list of celebrities, all of whom once appeared on The Love Boat.

He's the cute one.

Dan and **Tom** are former editors and writers for Malibu and Marvel Comics, and they have also written for the TV series *Malcolm in the Middle* and *Rugrats*. They've been story editors on *Pet Alien,* and on Nickelodeon's *Brothers Flub.*

Their combined height is twelve feet, one inch.

P.S. And they still read comic books!